MW01070447

Printed in the United States of America

First Printing, 2014

ISBN -9781503389106

Kid Kikel Productions Inc.
Tampa Florida

The Wild Adventures

Of

Chuck Kikel

A Short Story Trilogy

Blood on the High Seas

Chuck Kikel

Printed in the United States of America

First Printing, 2014

ISBN -9781503389106

Kid Kikel Productions Inc.
Tampa Florida

Dedicated to Douglas....this is all your fault

The Wild Adventures

Of

Chuck Kikel

Book One – Blood on the High Seas

Chuck Kikel

CHAPTER 1-- The Boys

Am I in my cabin dreaming?
Or are you really scheming
To take my ship away from me?
You'd better think about it
I just can't live without it
So please don't take my ship from me

I can feel the hand of a stranger
And it's tightening around my throat

Heaven help me
Heaven help me
Take this stranger from my boat
I'm your captain
I'm your captain

"I'm Your Captain" --- Grand Funk Railroad – 1970

Woodbridge New Jersey, September, 1976

To seventeen and eighteen year old boys, even ten minutes can seem like a lifetime, especially when something as important as a fishing trip is on the horizon. So last week felt like an eternity to me and my friends since last Saturday we had decided that if the weather was alright, we would hook up with a party boat out of Point Pleasant and do some fishing for both bluefish and stripers.

After what seemed like a never ending week of math, history, and Woodshop I, II, and III, Friday finally rolled around. The forecast for Saturday was perfect. Typical Northeast autumn weather: mid 60's to low 70's with a slight breeze out of the West. As the old saying goes, "Winds from the East, fishing's the least, winds from the West, fishing's the best!" We were pumped.

That night I called my buddies to make sure everything was

good to go for Saturday's trip aboard the party boat, *The Summer Wind*. I called my best friend,

Joe Pensipine,first. "Hey man, it's Chuck; you ready for tomorrow?" I asked.

"Why certainly," he answered. I think he was trying to impersonate Curly from *The Three Stooges*, but to me he sounded more like Barney Fife from *The Andy Griffith Show*.

"Cool man," I said, and then added, "I'll call Delerenzo, Miller, Waters and O'Grady as soon as we hang up. Just make sure you don't forget any of our shit." By shit I meant sandwiches and the usual junk food and drinks needed for a successful fishing trip. Joe's father, Joe Senior, owned a small grocery store in Colonia called Joe's Grocery Store. So naturally, Joe Junior was in charge of the eats. I called everyone else and made sure they all were still in. Everything went well until I called Kellen O'Grady.

"Hey man, it's Chuck. Ready?" I asked, as Kellen answered the phone.

"No man, not ready" he answered dejectedly.

"What do you mean no? Ain't ya going?" I asked.

"Can't Chuck, my mom won't let me. Some asshole prisoner broke out of jail tonight, and my mom won't let me go."

Now I knew that Kellen's father was a guard at Rahway Prison, but I didn't know why that meant that Kellen couldn't go fishing the next day. So I asked, "What's

that got to do with the price of tea in China?" To which Kellen answered, "Everything. My mom said whoever this guy is who escaped is a real nut job and very dangerous."

"So what?"

"So everything numnuts. You see, my father was going to be off tomorrow and he was going to watch my kid brother for my mom, cause she has some kind of doctor's appointment or something. So because my dad will have to work all night, he will probably be too tired to watch my brother and my mom said that I had to watch him instead."

Well, that was some pretty bad news for Kellen, but not that bad for me and my friends. You see, Kellen was fat, which is why we all used to tease him, by saying, "What the hellin are you eating Kellen?" Which always pissed him off. The rest of us were in really pretty good shape, if I do say so myself, but Kellen was always holding us up, taking forever to get anywhere and always being the first guy to get tired and wanting to call it quits. It's not that we didn't like him, we did. He was a nice kid with a good sense of humor, but his weight was always a pain in the ass for the rest of us. So Kellen not being able to go, really would not ruin the trip for the rest of us. Besides, he had just joined our group about two years earlier, while the rest of us have been together since the third grade, when I moved to Woodbridge.

Now when I say that the rest of us were in pretty good shape, I mean athletically speaking. Pensipine, Marty Delerenzo, and I were all on the varsity football team. Joe and I were running backs, and Marty, being the biggest of us all at 6 foot three and 240 pounds of pure muscle, was both an offensive and defensive monster.

Then there were Jimmy Waters and Johnny Miller, both of whom were on the varsity baseball team. Jimmy Waters played center field and had a good arm, but sometimes he could miss the broad side of a barn. On the other hand, with an arm like a canon, but with pinpoint accuracy to compliment that strength, Johnny Miller was a starting pitcher and batting champ. Out of all of us, Miller was the real athlete. He was all-state pitcher, and there were even scouts from Major League Baseball checking him out. So athletically, yeah, we were a solid group.

Now mentally and socially, well that was a different story. I guess Joe and I were the most "normal," or sensible. We got pretty good grades, we both had girlfriends our parents liked, and both planned on going to college. Joe was funny and nice. He wasn't slapstick or class clown funny, he was situational funny. By that I mean, no matter what the circumstances or situation, that guy always had something funny to say. He is the kind of guy that everyone seems to like instantly.

Marty Delerenzo was a pothead. Not that most kids didn't try pot, like at a party or camping or something but it was only occasional and nothing most kids couldn't live without (I think Joe and I were the only two seniors who didn't smoke). But Delerenzo, he smoked like a chimney. I can't remember a day he did not get high before school. "That's why they call it High School," Marty would joke. But other than that he was a really nice guy, except if someone messed with him when he was really high. Then all hell could break loose.

Waters was strange because he was introverted and especially afraid of girls. His parents were strict as hell and Jimmy became a fantastic liar in order to protect himself from a whipping. Other kids in school called him The Drip because of his last name and his weak personality, but none of us ever did. We really liked Jimmy and he was a

helluva good friend.

Johnny Miller was kind of boring because all he liked to do was practice or play ball. Pensipine and I were pretty sure he wasn't the sharpest tool in the shed. He never told any jokes; he never told any stories. In fact, probably the only thing he ever said that was remotely witty was "What's upchuck?" when he would greet me. It always gave him a giggle, it didn't for anyone else. But he did go out with the best looking girls in the school. Plus, if we were ever playing touch football or softball after school, we were almost guaranteed a win if Johnny Miller was on our team.

Basically, we were just your average group of New Jersey high school seniors, in September of 1976, about to embark on a journey that would change us for the rest of our lives.

CHAPTER 2-- The Captain

At this point the bottle was his only friend and the sea his only love. He lived less than five minutes from *The Summer Wind*. Unlike most of the other captains, Captain Jules Terwiliger didn't own his own head boat or party boat as they called them in Jersey. No, *The Summer Wind* belonged to a rich fellow named Clewiston who lived in Colts Neck, but had his practice in Belmar. Arnold Clewiston was a business attorney who sort of inherited the boat from a client who couldn't pay by any other means than to give up the ship, so to speak. Not being a seaman himself, nor having the time or desire to become a captain, Clewiston hired Jules Terwiliger.

That was three years ago today. And by all accounts Captain T was a good employee. He never missed a single day of work. He never called in sick. He was always on board at least a half hour before he needed to be, and he never had one complaint from a customer. The two to four mates who worked on *The Summer Wind* considered Captain T tough but fair, and for the most part they minded their own business and the captain minded his.

So this Friday evening, as Captain T sat with his half empty bottle of whiskey on his tattered old sofa in his crappy cluttered apartment, he took a swig of the sour mash and then looked at the gun. He had to chuckle to himself. What the fuck was he going to do with it? Shoot somebody? Rob somebody? Hold up a liquor store? What he did, was to pick up the .38 caliber Smith and Wesson and put the small snub nose in his mouth and pull the trigger. Click. He pulled it again. Click. And again. Click. At this point the captain became so hysterical with laughter that he actually fell off the couch, and pissed his pants. He thought of himself as the ultimate loser. For God's sake, he was such a loser that he couldn't even manage to kill himself. Suddenly he started choking, coughing, and sneezing, which he thought might cause him to have a heart attack, so he started laughing harder still. But in a few seconds the laughter turned to tears and he blacked out, sobbing.

Jules didn't dream that night, but if he had, it might have been about his wife Bev and his daughter Chrystal. On nights when he wasn't so drunk he did dream about them. The dream was always opposite of reality. In his dream they were still all together.

But his life changed when he woke up one morning five years earlier and found nothing in his home but a note. A note that told him how very sorry she was but that she and Chrystal deserved a better life than the odd jobs in odd ports and that she and their daughter needed stability in their lives and yak yak yak yak yak! *Bullshit*, he thought.

She was just like everybody else. At first she didn't care about possessions or money. It was all supposed to be about love and family. Bullshit with a capital B! All the whore cared about was money and things, things and money. He loved his wife but loved his daughter Chrystal more. So over the years his sadness turned to anger, and his anger to hate, and someday somebody was going to pay for all his suffering. Luckily it was at this point when he usually passed out and when he awoke in the morning, no one would ever know that he had been planning to do something really horrific the previous night.

CHAPTER 3-- Going to Work

The next morning Captain Jules Terwiliger woke up not remembering a thing from the night before. He took a quick shower, drank some stale coffee, put the gun in his backpack and went to work.

CHAPTER 4--The News Story

The Star Ledger

Saturday Edition   **$1.25**

Convicted Murderer Escapes NJ Prison

Rahway, N.J. Sep 16, 1976 (AP)

Rahway Police reported the escape of convicted murderer John Paul Jones at 6:45 pm yesterday. Authorities were using hounds and swat team members to comb the area for any signs of the escaped prisoner. Jones allegedly killed two prison guards during the escape. Authorities are not sure how Jones escaped the maximum security prison.

Police believe that Jones may be headed for the New Jersey shore area, stating he once lived in the Toms River section of Ocean County.

Jones was convicted of murdering a family of four including Don Peyote 49, his wife Lydia 44, son Edmund 17, and daughter

Deborah 15, in 1972. He was also convicted of murdering their neighbors Keith and Barbra Mulhale. Jones was sentenced to death for these crimes.

(Authors note: John Paul Jones is in no way related to the bass player of the rock group *Led Zeppelin* or the founder of the U.S. Navy. This is merely a coincidence.)

CHAPTER 5—Fishing

At 4 a.m. Saturday, everyone met at my house where we packed half our gear into my maroon '66 Chevy Impala, and the other half into Johnny Miller's pale blue and rust '72 Nova, and split for the shore. We took the Garden State Parkway all the way to exit 92, Brielle, and got off. It was another fifteen minutes until we entered the pot-holed parking lot of *The Summer Wind* party boat.

Legend had it that the boat got its name because Frank Sinatra allegedly won it from the boat's captain in an all night poker game. The legend also maintains that the boat's captain, Bear Nevil, was so drunk and crying so hard, that Sinatra let him have the boat back under one condition, that Bear rename the boat *The Summer Wind* and agree that if he ever sold it, the new owners would agree to keep the name. Captain Bear gladly accepted those terms. And even though the boat changed hands at least three times in the last decade, she is still known as *The Summer Wind.*

Even though it was only 6 a.m., there was a long line of fisherman boarding the boat. My friends and I were about half way back in line, but the line moved quickly, and in no time we staked our claim to five spots on the port side railing. Then, in a voice a little louder than I think he meant to use, Marty said, "Hey Chuck, we ought to start a gang called the blades" as he unleashed his hunting knife and thrashed it in the air. At first I didn't know what the hell he was talking about and figured it must be the marijuana speaking. I yelled at him to put the damn knife away before he got us kicked off the boat and he did. He was chuckling to himself as he did it. Then I noticed what he was talking about. All five of us wore the same type of hunting knife in the same type of a brown leather sheath, hanging off our belts on our left hips. To tell the truth, we did look kind of silly and I chuckled to myself.

We were about mid ship, got ourselves situated, and before we knew it, we were under way. The next forty-five minutes or so went quickly as we motored to our first spot. While we were cruising toward the first location where Captain Terwiliger would anchor,

Marty Delerenzo and I broke open the cooler and started eating some of the sandwiches Joe had brought for lunch. Marty must have had the munchies because I knew he had been smoking pot in Miller's Nova on the way down. But me, I was just hungry because I had been up since 2 a.m. I was so excited I couldn't fall back to sleep after I woke up to take a piss.

As we were swallowing the last bites of our sandwiches, we heard the hum of the big motors slowing down and waited with eager anticipation for one of the mates to call "lines down!" And seconds later, they did. All at once every one of the forty or so patrons simultaneously lowered their rigs to the salty depths below. The water had a little chop and there was a mild breeze. The sun was just starting to show and already we heard the first cry of "fish on" from the stern of the boat. My clam strip had just gotten about ten feet down when Wham! My rod struck the white, paint-chipped handrail with a lightning crash. As if on cue, Joe's rod, then Marty's, then Johnny's, and finally, Jimmy's rods were all bent in synchronicity. Pandemonium had broken loose. There were only two mates on board and as fast as they could, they were unhooking and marking 7-12 pound bluefish for the cooler.

As suddenly as it started, the bite ended. Dead. For approximately fifteen minutes, if you threw a coat hanger in the water you would have caught a fish. But now the ocean was as calm as a lake as the remaining fish headed off into the cold dark depths of the Atlantic. I asked one of the mates when he walked by, how many blues we had caught, and he said he wasn't sure, but the total for the boat was around seventy fish, the largest being a monster of over twenty pounds.

Another five minutes of waiting to see if any more fish would come by, and then one of the mates yelled "lines in!" I know this sounds crazy, but if there were bleachers out in the ocean and people were sitting in those bleachers watching our boat as the mate yelled "lines in," our audience would probably think they were watching some strange type of Broadway show dance. All at once, in perfect tandem, and in one continuous sweeping motion, all forty or so fisherman raised their rods out of the water and put them in the rod holders. It was like watching the Radio City Rockettes, for crying out loud, except that instead of beautiful, hot chicks in short dresses all kicking their legs so high you could see their assets, we were a bunch of unshaven, half asleep, blue jean and sweat- shirted men, between fifteen and ninety and years old, having the time of our lives.

CHAPTER 6 -- The Next Two Spots

So the motors kicked on and we started to roll. Pensipine and I grabbed some Yodels and Cokes, Johnny Miller had a bologna and cheese, Waters went to the head, and Delerenzo, well, we couldn't decide if he was staring off into space, sleeping, or dead. We hopped it was one of the first two choices, because we figured the weed was strong enough to put him in a daze, or make him fall asleep, but not kill him. It turned out to be the daze, because when he heard the cooler lid slam, he sauntered on over for some junk to quench his munchies.

Within ten minutes we were at our next spot and the Broadway show began again as the mates yelled "lines down!" Well, this spot was absolutely dead--so dead that Delerenzo actually fell asleep with his fishing rod in his hand. Within two seconds all my friends were rolling with laughter and pretty soon the entire boat was laughing. A couple minutes more of laughing and not a single fish and the mates yelled "lines up!"

That was the great thing about a party boat, if there were no fish biting, the captain would just haul anchor and be on his way to his next spot. More times than not, at least some of these spots were somewhat productive. And sometimes, if you were very lucky, they were very productive.

We cruised another few minutes to a new spot, where again nothing happened. So after ten minutes, it was anchors up, Broadway dance, lines in, and off to the next destination.

CHAPTER 7-- Arnold Clewiston, Don Peyote and

John Paul Jones (June 8, 1970)

Arnold Clewiston just returned to his office feeling like a million bucks. He thought to himself, *"How many other people get to change their clothes, walk out of their office, walk down the block to Ocean Avenue, and jog for five miles along the beautiful Atlantic Ocean?"* He had just taken a shower in the bathroom down the hall from his law office and was changing from shorts and sneakers back into his grey Armani suit.

As he sat back into the luxurious high-back Italian leather chair, the voice came over the speaker, "Mr. Clewiston, your two o'clock is here."

"Show him in," said Clewiston.

Little did Arnold Clewiston know that the meeting he was about to have would have such an enormous impact not only on him, but would end up being the catalyst of one of the most bizarre and heinous criminal events in New Jersey history. The funny thing was, most people would never know who Arnold Clewiston was. They would never know of this meeting. All they would talk about were the murders. And not just the murders that happened in the Peyote household and their unfortunate neighbors the Mulhales, but the grotesque murders that happened ten miles off the coast of Point Pleasant New Jersey, six years later, in September of 1976.

You see, three years earlier, in 1967, Don Peyote was about to realize a dream come true. Even though he had been a roofer by trade for 26 years, Peyote had always dreamed of owning a sports bar. He had always supposed this to be a pipe dream, until the day John Paul Jones's grandmother hired him to put a new roof on her home. Her husband of 46 years had just passed away and she needed to put a new roof on her home

so she could sell it and move to Florida where her sister lived.

One day while working on her roof, Peyote stopped for a break, and started talking with Mrs. Jones. He found out that her husband had left their business to their only grandson. The business was called *The End Zone*, and was a very successful watering hole located on Route 35 in Neptune. The only problem was that the grandson, John Paul Jones, was recently released from prison for selling cocaine. In New Jersey, the law doesn't allow anyone with a criminal record to have a liquor license, so her grandson was desperately seeking someone he could trust whose name he could put the sports bar in, which would allow him to secretly continue to own the business.

A short time later, the two men met and rapidly agreed to an illegal deal. In exchange for his life's savings ($100,000), Don Peyote would be the sole owner of *The End Zone*, and John Paul Jones would be the business manager. That was how it would appear on paper only. The real arrangement was, Don Peyote would give John Paul Jones $50,000 and get 10% of the business. He also would be in charge of all the daily operations. Jones would basically own 90% of the bar and be hands off. This not-well-thought- out plan was agreed to and started two months from the date of the agreement. Both parties had gotten what they wanted. Don Peyote got to own and run a sports bar, and John Paul Jones did nothing at all and collected a bundle of money.

And everything turned out surprisingly well until Peyote started getting uneasy and then flat out frightened. Around two and a half years into the agreement, John Paul Jones was getting out of control. His cocaine habit was back, he was dealing again, and more than once he was escorted out of *The End Zone* for starting fights with customers. Peyote was afraid Jones would get arrested again and the shit would hit the fan. When Don told his wife Lydia about his concerns, she made things even worse. She was a very nervous person by nature and loved to panic. She convinced Don that not only would he lose his part of the bar and his income, but he would probably end up in jail for his illegal agreement with Jones.

So it was Lydia who made the fatal error of convincing her husband to meet with the attorney Arnold Clewiston and see if he could help them out of their contract with Jones. Don Peyote wanted to get out of the contract. He wanted his initial investment of $50,000 back, plus another $250,000 compensation for the time he put in, not only keeping the bar running, but actually growing in profits. He would use this money, plus the $50,000 he had in savings as a down payment to start his own sports bar.

After Arnold Clewiston listened to Peyote's plan, he told him it would not be easy to accomplish for many reasons. First, the actual agreement between Peyote and Jones was illegal. Second, putting a value on what his contributions were worth was arbitrary and Jones would fight it. Third, who knew if Jones had that kind of cash available. Clewiston told Peyote that it would be very hard, but not impossible. He said that his fees were high, and that he was afraid that his fees would use up a lot of the money he could recover. Peyote had already thought about that and offered Clewiston a Party Boat called *The Summer Wind,* that he recently inherited from his father, but really had no use for and was looking to sell. Clewiston agreed to take the boat for payment, and proceeded with the case.

CHAPTER 8-- John Paul Jones's Head Explodes

The second John Paul opened the letter from Clewiston's office his head exploded. His immediate thought was, *"that mother-fucker!"* While Jones was by no means a calm, rational person to begin with, when you added mounds of cocaine to the equation, well, you had a human time bomb. His mind raced as fast as his car. Within minutes of reading the affidavit, he grabbed his gun, a knife, and an armful of rope and headed for Peyote's house. He made sure he did a few lines of coke before he left, just to keep himself sharp. As he raced toward his destination, his thoughts were flying.

He would lose the bar. He would probably be arrested. He would be broke. All because his asshole partner wanted to muscle him out of his own money. *"Never friggin' happening. I will kill you where you stand, you ungrateful piece of shit."* These were the kind of thoughts going through his head.

When he got to the Peyote house, he parked in the driveway, did two more generous lines of coke, grabbed the knife and the gun (he forgot about the rope), and walked to the front door.

CHAPTER 9-- The Peyotes' Last Day on Earth

John Paul Jones' eyes were as red and glassy as Dracula's as he rang the doorbell. No matter how many times his mother had told him to always ask who was at the door before opening it as he was growing up, Don Peyote just opened the door. It was the last thing he ever did.

As soon as their eyes met, John Paul's rage exploded. Without a moment's hesitation, and without really thinking, he pointed the .357 magnum directly at Peyote's eye and pulled the trigger. The bullet entered his right eye socket and made a hole approximately the same size. The back of his head was a different story. The entire back of his head from the crown to the nape of his neck was completely blown off. Jones was actually amazed at how far his scalp and brains flew across the living room. Chunks of his brain stuck to the TV screen fifteen feet away as the red and grey masses slowly started racing each other to the bottom of the tube. Finally, the grey matter, which used to hold Mr. Peyote's thoughts, dropped to the hardwood floor. John Paul Jones had never felt more alive in his life.

At the sound of the cacophony in the living room, the two Peyote children, Edmund and Deborah, along with their mother Lydia, came running from their separate bedrooms into the living room. Three shots and three seconds later Don Peyote's family joined him on the floor. Edmund and Deborah were lucky. Edmund was hit in the heart and Deborah in the lung. Both died in seconds. But Lydia was not so lucky. Her bullet hit much lower, going straight into her right hip. Molten flames of pain darted through her body. Her head smacked the hardwood floor hard as she fell, but unfortunately, not hard enough to knock her out. Her eyes widened but no sound came from her mouth as she tried to scream. She looked like a fish out of water gasping for its next breath. As Jones drew nearer, her bladder released as she saw the huge blade being withdrawn from his waistband. He started to kneel on top of her and her arms and fists flew wildly of their own volition. Jones took the butt end of the knife and crashed it into her skull. Although still conscious, her arms fell to the floor. He ripped open her blouse, exposing her breasts, and thought, *"what a lucky guy Peyote was."* Then he raised his right arm as high as he could and drove the blade thru her breastplate and into her heart.

John Paul made no attempt whatsoever to clean up his mess or cover his tracks. Besides a tiny bit of blood on his right hand, from Mrs. Peyote's heart, there wasn't a mark on Jones. He licked the blood off, thought it tasted salty, got into his car and started to drive away. Then he noticed the Peyotes' neighbors, Keith and Barbra Mulhale watching him from their porch. They had no idea what had just happened and were lost in conversation, when a car stopped in front of their home. They really paid no attention, assuming it was a lost soul looking for directions. John Paul Jones walked up to the porch, pulled out his gun and shot them both in the face.

He could have probably gotten away with the murders for a little while at least, because there were no witnesses. But in a stroke of unbelievably bad luck, a police cruiser had just coincidentally turned onto the block, and the officers saw Jones

cold bloodedly kill the Mulhales. They screeched their cruiser to a

halt, drew their weapons, and ordered Jones to drop his weapon.

He did.

CHAPTER 10-- The Third and Final Spot

As we approached our third spot, Joe and I were both

feeling like our luck was about to change. How little did we know

how right we were, but not for the reasons we thought. We

thought the fishing was about to explode, and once again our arms

would hurt from pulling fish in. Why in the world would it cross our

minds, even for a second, that a bloodbath nightmare was only

moments away?

"It's a shame that not only am I going to be catching more fish than you, but also bigger fish!" I said, boasting my machismo and challenging my friend.

"Is that right?" answered Joe. "Well I got a finsky here that says I'll catch more fish than you, and another five bucks that says I'll also catch a bigger fish than you!" bragged a proud Pensipine.

"It will be a pleasure taking your ten dollars." I said with confidence.

The big motors slowly began to idle. As the anchors were lowered, once again the cries of "lines down" echoed from bow to stern and once again the Broadway dance began. When I looked toward the bow, I noticed that Miller and Waters were talking. Then for a split second I started to worry. *"Where the heck was Delerenzo?"* As that thought was still fresh in my mind I felt Joe's elbow catch me in the ribs. I looked to where he was pointing and found Delerenzo. The big boy was sound asleep on the bench behind his fishing rod. The combination of good pot, good food, the motion of the ocean and fresh air had gently seduced our enormous friend into the Twinkie zone.

Since the action started out slowly, our conversation switched to one of our other favorite topics, music. "Chuck, did Delerenzo tell you he got us three tickets for the Paul McCartney concert at the Garden?" asked Joe.

"No way, that show sold out in fifteen minutes. Delerenzo and I waited in line all night at Jack's Music shop in Redbank, and it sold out way before we got to the window."

So Joe adds, "Yeah, Jack's is usually the best place to buy tickets. Jack is cool, unlike Ticketmaster that punches out one ticket at a time, as each customer requests them. Then, they ring up the order and ten minutes can go by and they have only punched out two tickets. Jack just starts printing the tickets out as fast as he can as soon as they go on sale. He gets the best seats that way. Then when the show is sold out, he has a pile of great seats that he sells to whoever is on line at his back window. If you're lucky enough to be close to the front of the line, you can get amazing tickets.

"Remember we got fourth row tickets for Zeppelin and tenth row seats for *The Who*?"

"Not to mention the great seats for Jethro Tull, David Bowie and Dylan," I added excitedly. "So how did he get seats for McCartney?"

Joe says, "There's this new store on Main Street in Woodbridge called MDM Tickets. It's run by these three burn out guys, and they always seem to have great tickets to any show, *after* the show has sold out. The tickets cost a lot of money, but they are well worth it. I don't know who they have to kill to get them, but somehow they always seem to get them."

And I ask, "How much did they cost and where are they located?"

"They cost forty dollars each and they're sixth row center on the floor," he answers.

"Forty dollars each! Holy crap Batman, that is a ton of cash. The face value on those were what, about ten bucks?" I asked in disbelief.

"Yeah, yeah, sure those guys are getting rich, but who cares, sixth row center for McCartney, he's a Beatle for God's sake," he said as he playfully hit me in the shoulder.

"I guess your right" I agreed.

Our conversation was about to continue when Pensipine said, "Holy shit! Did you hear that?" Of course I heard it. It sounded as if someone were blowing up fire crackers on the other side of the boat. Bang! Then a short while later... bang! Then, bang! again.. Our heads whipped around to search for the mates. They were nowhere in sight.

"I feel sorry for the poor bastard who did that." said Joe.

"I know what you mean. Remember last year when those kids blew up the M-80's on our fishing trip? They were screwed. The mates confiscated their fishing gear and made them sit in the galley the entire trip. I remember one of the kids was puking his guts up because that happens if it gets rough and you are forced to sit inside."

And Joe says, "I bet it was those three kids I saw on the other side of the boat. I hope they enjoyed themselves, because judging how tough the mates looked, those guys are in deep shit." Little did we know, but we were the ones about to be in deep shit.

After a few more minutes, and not a single fish being brought over the gunwale, I say to Pensipine, "We've been here an awful long time without so much as a nibble. I hope Captain T has the good sense to leave soon and find a better spot." Now everyone is grumbling.

"Do you think maybe the mates are having trouble with those kids and that's why we're not moving?" asked Joe.

"What kids? What trouble?" asked a wobbly and newly awakened Delerenzo.

"Good morning, Miss, did you enjoy your nappy nap?" laughed Joe. At this point, Mike Delerenzo wrapped Joe Pensipine in his mammoth arms, giving him a bone

crushing bear hug. Even though Pensipine was in good shape, he was no match for the enormous Delerenzo. In seconds Joe's face started turning red, so I yelled, "put him down ya big ape," which Delerenzo did instantly as if I were his drill sergeant.

"What the hell is wrong with you, ya big monkey?" Joe asked as soon as he got his wind back.

"Geez, can't a guy have a little fun? C'mere ya big baby, Daddy still loves you." said Mike as he grabbed Joe around the neck and gave Joe a knuckle burner to the scalp.

The two finally broke apart and Delerenzo asked, "So what the hell is going on? Why are we just sitting here? What kids? Is there anything left to eat?" Damn munchies.

"I think I'll go up and check with the Captain to see what's going on. We're burning daylight." I said.

"Yeah, go kick his ass Chuck" said Delerenzo.

"Tell him we are not on a sightseeing cruise" added Pensipine.

So I put my rod in my holder and walked to the middle of the boat until I got to the stairway. The stairs were old, creaky, narrow and painted white with a blue trim to match the rest of the boat. There was a one inch tubular iron handrail that was cold to the touch. As the stairs ascended, they curved around to the left, almost like a backward 'C.' As I was approaching the top of the stairs I realized how quiet everything was. I don't know why, but I just had a feeling that something wasn't right. Usually I would hear seagulls screeching or something, but it was eerily quiet. My heartbeat was a little fast and I tried to convince myself that it was because I had just climbed the steps. I also realized as I was climbing upwards that everything seemed to be slowing down. Each step was long and deliberate.

Finally, I was on the top landing and facing the door to the wheelhouse. The door was narrow, and though freshly painted to match the rest of the boat, you could tell it was very old. The wood was splintering and the small eyelevel window was so aged and yellowed that it was impossible to make out anything inside. I rapped my knuckles on the old wooden door and waited for an answer. Nothing. I knocked again harder, and again nothing. I started to push open the door when I noticed the tiniest speck of red, right where I had placed my hand. I swallowed hard and proceeded into the wheelhouse.

My first thought when I entered the tiny room was that I was in the haunted mansion in Longbranch. All the angles seemed strange and out of proportion. The three big windows directly in front of me were covered with sea mist, both old and new. They let in a lot of light and in spite of that the rest of the room was dark. There were red streaks randomly splattered across the three panels, with the thickest and darkest red in the center pane, thinning out more and more as it spread its pattern outward towards the edges of the other two windows. There were black chunks of hair and chunks of grayish pink globs of what appeared to be jellylike in texture, also following the pattern of the red streaks. In a few spots randomly around the center window were what looked like yellowish white *Chiclets* imbedded in the glass. The instrument panel and the rest of the structure in the wheelhouse were of some ancient looking, yet handsome, wood.

The body was slumped over the big wheel that steers the boat. The back of the man's head looked like someone had taken a hair dryer to it but didn't finish the job. The hair was parted in the middle, with a small black round hole in the center of it. Out of the hole oozed dark red syrup, that was already starting to dry as it ran down the man's neck. His arms were hanging down at his sides and my first thought was that he looked like one of my friends who had passed out drunk at a party.

Suddenly, I felt lightheaded as the reality of what I was looking at started to register in my mind. Without thinking, I put my arm on the doorjamb to prevent myself from falling. My knees had grown week and my stomach was starting to flip. My mind raced.

Apparently, someone had recently snuck up behind the captain and

shot him point blank in the back of the head. But why? I had no

idea. What I did know was that what I was looking at was his blood,

hair, teeth and brains splattered on the windows and console. I

thought back to the explosions Joe and I had heard earlier. They

were not firecrackers; they were gunshots. But how many? I

couldn't remember. Two, maybe three; I wasn't sure. So where

were the other bullets? It appeared as if the captain was hit only

once, but I couldn't be sure. I damn well wasn't going to start

poking his body or moving him to look. At the same time, the

thought occurred to me that whoever did this must still be on the

boat. You might think that this was the moment when panic set in.

But it wasn't. After my initial bout of queasiness, I regained my

composure. I don't know why, but I have this gift. For example,

there were times when those around me turned to a massive bowl

of Jello, when things got out of control. Like the time my little

cousin Mikey cut his foot off when my uncle was mowing the lawn.

Mikey was playing running bases with some other kids, and as he was trying to slide into base, he missed, and slid right under the lawn mower my uncle was pushing. My uncle passed out cold;

my aunt went hysterical crying, and I ran into the house, filled a bucket with ice, ran out and put the foot into the bucket, tied my shirt around Mickey's little leg to stop the bleeding, and drove him and his foot to the emergency room. Sixteen hours later and the foot was successfully reattached to my cousin. As I walked into the recovery room, all the doctors, nurses, other patients and all the people in my family started to sing "For he's a jolly good fellow," to me.

But back to the captain. I was pretty sure he was dead but wanted to be positive. I grabbed him around the shoulders and tried to turn him so I could listen for a heart beat or just see if he was breathing. The weight of his head on his limp body just rolled around and immediately I knew it would be unnecessary to take a pulse. Although there was just a small hole in the back of his head where the bullet had entered, his entire face was blown apart from the bullet exiting. What was once his face, now looked like burnt

Spaghetti O's only a much deeper, darker red than the orange tint

of *Spaghetti O's* sauce. The captain's exploded face was more the

color of a piece of pizza around the edges between where the

cheese ends and the crust begins. The captain's body slipped

through my hands and hit the hardwood floor with a double thud.

First his body, "thud," then his head, "thud." Okay, he was dead.

I noticed the door on the opposite side of the wheelhouse

was slightly ajar with something preventing it from closing. I

stepped over the captain and opened the door. There, lying on the

floor, in what at first glance appeared to be a lovers' embrace, were

the two mates. Their bodies were wrapped around each other, but

judging from the amount of blood and lack of movement, I figured

they had met the same fate as the captain. There was no need to

examine these two, thank you very much. They were dead.

I figured the first thing I should do was call for help. So I

headed back into the wheelhouse, stepped over Captain Spaghetti

O and grabbed the ship-to-shore radio microphone. I depressed the lever and started calling out "SOS." A few seconds later and someone was on the other end instructing me what channel the Coast Guard monitored, so I switched to that. An official sounding voice asked what the problem was and I told him all about Captain Spaghetti O and his fatally entwined mates. The voice on the other end told me to remain calm and to read him our bearings. Using his guidance, I found the instruments with our latitude and longitude bearings. He told me to hide, and wait for their arrival. I dropped the microphone and started running to get back to my friends. I couldn't hide and wait. What would happen to my friends if I did not get back to warn them and help them? What about the rest of the passengers? I didn't know exactly what I had to do, but I knew I had to do something.

As I reached the bottom step my heart sank as I looked to the stern and there was no one there. Was I too late? Were they all dead already? Were the bodies all tossed overboard by some madman and left for the sharks? No; as I snapped my head around to the front of the boat, I saw that everyone was huddled in a huge crowd. In the center of the crowd were all my friends. I crouched down and snuck up on the crowd. Then I managed to make my way to the center and stood between Pensipine and Delerenzo. As I looked toward the very front of the boat, there to my shock and amazement, waving a gun, was the captain.

CHAPTER 11-- Mother Fucking Clewston

John Paul Jones never felt one second of regret for the Peyote - Mulhale murders. *That son of a bitch Don Peyote double crossed him and he got what he had coming to him,* he thought. As far as the rest of the victims? Anyone who is friends with an asshole like Peyote also gets what they deserve. But that's not what occupied Jones's time or deranged scheming mind while he was in prison. He had one more double crossing asshole to deal with. You see, the murders were so gross and so heinous, the media couldn't get enough of the story. So John Paul's cell was loaded with articles about the infamous incident. And for weeks, while the trial was going on, that media whore, Arnold "The Jew Lawyer," as Jones referred to him, Clewiston, was on every news show, magazine and newspaper imaginable, soaking up every bit of the limelight. And he never failed to mention that Don Peyote paid him off with some stupid fishing boat down in Point Pleasant, *The Summer Wind. The Summer Wind. The Summer Wind . . .*

CHAPTER 12-- The Final (GULP!) Chapter

So it boils down to this: me, Pensipine, Delerenzo, Waters and Miller -- five high school kids from central Jersey, surrounded by approximately forty other assorted fisherman, also presumably from New Jersey, all awaiting our fates. We were being held hostage, stuck floating on the Atlantic Ocean, on this very strange, autumn day.

I realized two critical things. One, I needed to find out what the hell was going on here, and two... Time was of the essence. So I whisper to my best friend Joe Pensipine, "Joe, What the hell is going on here?"

"Thank God you're back Chuck. I'm not sure what's going on, but what I can gather from the babbling captain is this..."

So quietly and quickly Joe told me how the captain was drunk as a skunk and rambling on about how no one was ever going to take his ship from him, not no one, not no how. And if we didn't believe him, just go ask the dead stowaway driving the boat. Not only that, but the captain also made it clear that none of us were to be trusted, especially not his dear old wife, who took his daughter away, or the stowaway who tried to take his boat away. He said he was going to kill us all one by one to make damn sure no one would betray him again. He also rambled on about the last thing to go through the stowaway son of a bitches' mind before he died was a bullet. Great. That's all I needed. Not only was this madman about to kill us all, but he was a rotten comedian to boot.

So let's recap for clarity. First, there's a dead guy in the wheelhouse, who I thought was the captain, but who was actually a stowaway, who had apparently been planning on killing the real captain and stealing his boat. Next, there were the two dead mates on the stairs, who the stowaway had killed *before* he was ambushed in the wheelhouse by the drunken captain. And finally, we have the captain, who, as it turns out, is a nutcase, sneaking up on the stowaway in the wheelhouse, and turning the tables on said stowaway (and prison escapee, which I didn't learn until much later) by killing him first.

So, I am letting all this new info sort itself out in my head, when Pensipine says, "Boys, it's time for Routine Six."

"What the hell is routine six?" asked Miller and Waters in harmony, which was exactly the same question I was asking myself.

"I don't know, but that's what the Bowery Boys always said in a time like this. It seems they always had a pre-arranged plan for every dangerous situation that ever came up, no matter how bizarre the situation. So, Slip, or Satch, would yell out "Routine Six," and all the Bowery Boys would know exactly what to do," Pensipine explained.

We all looked at each other as if Martians had just landed on our boat, and were it not for the seriousness of the situation, I think we would have laughed ourselves silly. Typical Pensipine -- no matter what the situation, he tried to make it comical.

Then, just as I am about to start making up my own Routine Six, the drunken Captain T tells the passenger closest to him to step over to where he was standing. The man was about six feet tall, appeared to be in his mid 40's and also appeared to be alone. He stepped over next to Captain Terwilliger, and without warning, the good captain shot him directly in the forehead. The back of his head and bits of his skull showered the people in the front of the crowd, closest to the captain. As the man fell his bladder and bowels both released themselves. His dead body lay in a heap at Terwilliger's feet. Two people in the very front started vomiting, and the captain immediately executed them both. People were screaming, shaking and vomiting all over the place. I needed to make a split second decision.

I huddled up my friends and told them, "Okay guys, it's Routine Six time." Joe Pensipine had a big stupid smile on his face, but the rest looked at me with dead serious expressions, as if I were the Burning Bush about to address Moses. Instead, I explained the plan. "When I count to three, I want Marty Delerenzo to start walking calmly toward the captain, saying loudly but gently, 'Excuse me captain, but I could use your help.' Just keep doing that. I think it will take him by such surprise, that he will forget to shoot you. I hope. Besides, it is a natural human reflex to try to help anyone who asks for help -- nicely. So I'm counting on the fact that between the surprise and his natural instincts we can buy a few seconds. While Captain T is busy with you, the rest of us will pull our knives out and throw them at the Captain."

"Then what?" asked Waters, with his eyes bulging out of his head.

"Then what, what?" I asked. Again, I almost lost control of myself and had to fight the urge to laugh uncontrollably.

"Then we'll probably all die. If we don't die, then we'll go right into Routine Seven" said Joe.

This time we all did start laughing. You know how it is, like when you're at a funeral and all of a sudden the laughter just takes over and there is nothing you can do about it.

So here we all are, seconds away from being executed by a madman, and we're all laughing like a bunch of hyenas.

"What the hell is going on over there?" Captain Terwilliger shouted as he started making his way towards us.

"Excuse me Captain, but I was wondering if you could help me out?" asked Delerenzo, his cheeks wet from tears which came from his nervous laughter.

"What did you say?" asked a very perplexed and drunk Captain T. Before Marty could get the entire sentence out I yelled, "Now!"

I'll never forget what happened next. It all seemed to happen in slow motion. Waters' was the first knife to fly. I could see it tumble end over end until it struck an old man in the front of the crowd, smack in the middle of his thigh. Remember, Waters had a strong arm but had trouble with accuracy. The man let out a scream and the captain's head whipped around to see what the commotion was about. The old man fell to the ground. Captain T raised his gun in our general direction but it was too late. Miller's knife was there before he could squeeze off a round, and the blade struck solidly into the captain's right wrist. Blood was spurting out like a fountain.

The captain did not drop the gun though; because he couldn't. The

ligaments in his wrist were severed and his fingers were as useless

as tits on a bull. As I released my knife, I could follow its trajectory

with radar precision. I watched as it tumbled end over end in slow

motion until the razor sharp steel blade went through Captain

Terwilleger's chest, broke a bone, and pierced his heart. Pensipine

must have been in shock, because by time he threw his weapon,

the captain lay dead on the floor. Joe's knife sailed harmlessly out

to sea.

EPILOGUE

I don't want to bore you with lots of details about what happened between the time we realized that Captain Jules Terwiliger was dead and the time we got back to the dock of *The Summer Wind*. Who really knows, because most of what happened at that time is very fuzzy in my memory. I mean I couldn't tell you if it were real or urban legend, but, folks say that some of the passengers were so outraged at the demented drunken captain, that they cut his fingers off and used them for bait until the Coast Guard finally showed up to tow us in. Some even say that Delerenzo was the one who instigated the whole thing. But I couldn't tell you.

All I really remember was sitting at the back of *The Summer Wind* and watching the beautiful water V out behind us. I remember filling my lungs with fresh, sweet smelling saltwater air. I remember thinking it was great to be alive. I guess I fell into a trance until I felt myself being hoisted onto the shoulders of the tremendous crowd gathered at the dock to give us a hero's welcome.

As I lay in my bed that night, drifting off towards sleep, the last thing I remembered was the crowd singing to me as they carried me on their shoulders……"For he's a jolly good fellow, for he's a jolly good fellow, for he's a jolly good fellooow, which nobody can deny."

Bye for now…..Chuck Kikel

MarshMellows

Chuck Kikel

Printed in the United States of America
First Printing, 2014
ISBN -9781503389106
Kid Kikel Productions Inc.
Tampa Florida

Dedicated to Petey...

This is all your fault

BOOK 2

Marsh*mellows*

Chuck Kikel

October 23, 1977

Prelude I

Marshmallows. If someone were to ask me for the first word that comes into my mind when thinking about camping, it would be marshmallows. The word just seems to flow off the tongue. Marshmallows. Of course I could say a word like 'campfires' or 'stars' or 'hiking' or 'fishing.' But no, for me the first word that comes to mind is... marshmallows. "Why Chuck, do you think of marshmallows?" you might ask, and my answer would be simple. Marshmallows tie the entire trip together. The first thing I do when I make plans to go camping is put together a list of what I will need: tent, rope, grill, water purification system, toilet paper, various articles of clothing, maps, lighter, matches, binoculars, knife, hammer, sleeping bag, flashlight, food, fishing gear, water etc. etc. But the first thing I always put on my list is marshmallows. I keep a bag in my car for the ride to my camping destination. These are eaten raw and get me in the correct frame of mind for the adventures that will follow. There is something about the white, but almost invisible powder that engulfs the perimeter of a raw mallow.

So soft, yet so smooth. This is in great contrast to the center of the puffy morsel. The center is sticky, stretchy, gooey, and syrupy sweet. And however much I love this taste sensation; it pales in comparison to the magnificent *toasted* campfire marshmallow.

The toasted campfire marshmallow is the Michelangelo of junk food. It is indeed a work of art. It must be prepared perfectly. Too far away from the fire and it will never cook. Too close to the flame and it will actually catch on fire and the skin will turn an ashen, cancerous black. The trick is to keep it just the right distance from the heat source and to keep twirling the stick so that eventually the outer skin is a uniform golden brown. Underneath the skin there is a warm, light, shiny delicate morsel of melted white stuff. There is nothing better, at the end of a fabulous day of camping, when the air is cool and the leaves gently rustle, than to sit around the fire, gaze at the stars and eat perfectly toasted marshmallows.

Prelude II

Petey, (pronounced peetee) was just about the most beautiful girl in the universe. At seventeen years old, it should have been illegal to be that good looking. She had long, silky, dark brown hair, and her eyes were doe shaped and green -- not that horrible green some people have, (you know what I mean, the kind that makes them look like some comic book villain or a cat or something). No, these eyes could melt your heart. And her teeth were perfect, which doesn't mean that they were unnaturally white. Really white teeth can also look like shit. If your teeth are so big that Mr. Ed laughs at you, well, that stinks. And if you have little tiny teeth that look like tic-tacs, that stinks too. And don't even get me started on gums. Some girls have fairly nice teeth but their gums are so big you could build another Mount Rushmore on them. Petey's teeth were pearly white, straight and perfectly sized.

She was five foot ten and had a body that could stop traffic. She never wore a bra, always camisoles, and she said her boobs were the same size as Dolly Parton's. Well, not exactly. I think she may have exaggerated a teensy bit. I would say they were more like Sylvia Krystal's boobs (She was the sex kitten who starred in the original *Emmanuelle* films). Her legs went from here to there and back again, and were connected to an ass that could crack walnuts. And don't even get me started on her feet. I know this sounds crazy, but I fell in love with her feet before I even said one word to her.

The day we met was the first day for both of us at a part time clerical job for J & J. I was sitting alone in the cafeteria and happened to glance under the table across from me. She was wearing sandals. Oh my God, perfect feet. Everything about them was perfect. The toes were perfect. Not long and bony or crooked, yuck. Not short and fat and wrinkled, eek! No, they were just right, the perfect length and shaped toes. And her toenails were painted a candy apple red, which is also a perfect color for '69 corvettes. Her feet looked so soft and her heels were also just right. If you are a woman with dried, cracked heels, don't even try to talk to me. It won't happen. I swear to God it won't.

Anyway, when I looked up she was staring right at me. To

my horror she was getting up and it was obvious she was coming over to me.

"Hi, my name is Patricia, mind if I join you?" Holy crap, I thought; she was going to blast me for eyeing up her feet, but actually she just wanted company. To make an already too long prelude short, here is what happened. Although she was the most gorgeous creature I had ever seen, she was a big chicken. She had no self-confidence whatsoever. She was frightened to death to be all alone at this new job so she latched onto me like a barnacle to a piling. Six months went by; I stole her away from her boyfriend, and we have been living together ever since. That was almost two years ago.

Now that all of this prelude stuff is done, I can finally get onto the real story.

Chapter 1 -- On the Road

Petey was nowhere to be found. I had been up since 5a.m. and had already made three trips from our apartment to the parking lot. I stacked everything up against my royal blue '72 Nova. You could barely see the white racing stripes or the shining Craigar mag wheels. Man did we have a lot of gear. After my third trip, when I finally had everything outside, I packed it all into my trunk and the back seat. With all that finished, I returned to the apartment.

"Petey!" I yelled. I was in the kitchen so I figured either she was still asleep or taking a shower. Again, only a little louder and with a tiny bit more urgency, "Petey, where are you?" No reply. She was a pretty sound sleeper, so I was almost certain she had overslept. Besides, I didn't hear the shower running. When I walked into the bedroom I was surprised. The bed was made and everything was in place. If I didn't know better, I might think this was a guest room that no one ever used. Now my concern was growing. This was not like her. She was usually late for everything, so I fully expected to see her in bed. I started slowly down the hallway toward the white hall to the bathroom door on the right. Something just didn't feel right. If I were a German Shepherd, my ears would be standing straight up, eagerly scanning the silence for any telltale sign of life. I placed my hand on the knob, held my breath and began to gently turn the latch. Suddenly, my blood ran cold as I felt a hand squeeze my shoulder. My heart skipped as I whirled around and found myself standing eye to eye with Petey.

"Good morning, handsome," Petey said through her pretty smile.

"Wha, who, I mean where the heck were you?" I asked as I tried to gain my composure.

"I've got a surprise for you, Chuck. I know you forgot it's our anniversary, but I didn't and I've got some presents for you in the living room. I snuck out of the apartment and went over to Jenny's house where I have been hiding them."

I have to give credit to that girl, she was a hundred percent right, I *had* totally forgotten about our anniversary.

"Are you kidding me," I asked? "Me forget our anniversary? Never happen. Not in this lifetime. I'm just waiting for the perfect moment to give you your gift, that's all." I hoped she fell for it. It was lame and it was a stall tactic, but that's all I could come up with at that moment.

"Yeah, right Mr. Romance; you totally forgot," she answered. I grabbed her waist and gave her a playful squeeze as I followed her into the living room.

"So, what did you get me?" I asked as I started to unwrap the first of three presents. "Oh wow!" I exclaimed as I unwrapped a beautiful, leather-sheathed, carved bone handled, hunting knife. "Wow," I said again, "How did you remember?"

"How could I forget? It was only a little over a year ago when you saved all those peoples' lives down in Point Pleasant from that madman psycho killer Captain Terwilliger. I know the police let you keep the knife you threw at him that killed him instantly as it pierced through his black heart…"

"Okay, Okay, enough with the dramatics. Yes, I saved everyone, and yes I killed that fool with my old knife, but you don't have to get creepy with that black heart stuff. Anyway, I'm really touched that you remembered that I really didn't like using that knife anymore. This is a terrific present, and I love it almost as much as I love you."

The next gift was not exactly a surprise. I mean, it would be almost impossible to camouflage a fishing rod and reel with wrapping paper. I thanked her again and kissed her as I reached for my third and final anniversary present.

"Now what could this be?" I asked as I felt the small package below the wrapping paper. This time I couldn't guess. It felt like a pillow, but somehow softer.

"Oh, go ahead and open it ya' big bear," said Petey.

As I tore the gift wrap away a huge smile stretched across my face. I instantly recognized the orange and blue lettering over the snow white background. "Marshmallows," I laughed as the remaining shreds of paper fell away. We kissed and hugged and I reassured her I had not forgotten our anniversary and would present her with her gift at the correct time, whenever that was.

We locked up the apartment, and headed out on our adventure, marshmallows in hand.

Chapter 2 - - Just Lucky

Thank God I never finished opening the bathroom door.

Chapter 3 – The Guys

At the same time Petey was giving me my anniversary presents at my apartment, Joe Pensipine, Jimmy Waters, Johnny Miller, and Kellen O'Grady were a few miles away in Colonia, New Jersey, at Joe Pensipine's father's grocery store.

"I don't give a shit how much you love 'em, we're not bringing stuff to make smores," laughed my best friend Joe Pensipine, as he playfully smacked the rotund Kellen O'Grady on the back of his big red head with a bag of hamburger buns.

They were both gathering food for our camping trip. They didn't need to see over in the next aisle, to know who was attached to the two voices that rang out in perfect unison singing, "What the hellin' are you eaten,' Kellen?" because it was obvious it was their buddies Jimmy Waters and Johnny Miller. However, the harmonized insult fell on deaf ears. Kellen had heard it so many times before, that now his tunnel vision for the smores supplies was the only thing that mattered.

"Who died and left you king of the damn food supplies?" asked Kellen, the only member of our entire camping ensemble who was not on one of the high school sports teams last year. Pensipine, Marty Delorenzo, and I were on the football team and Waters and Miller were on the baseball team. My girlfriend Petey was also an athlete, as she was captain of the girls' swim team at Woodbridge High School.

"Nobody died, but we are in Joe's Grocery Store, which is named after Joe Pensipine Sr, which is who *I* am named after, and that makes *me* in charge, get it?" answered Joe. There is a definite pecking order amongst teenage boys and Joe Pensipine was at the top of the food chain, and poor Kellin O'Grady was at the polar opposite end.

The four friends finished their shopping, said goodbye to Joe's dad, and loaded up the car. With this task completed, two thirds of our caravan was in place. We were all going to drive an hour and a half, and meet at the Hotshops Rest Stop on the New York State Thruway. There we would grab something to eat, relieve our bladders and continue another hour to our final destination,

Ellenville, New York.

Chapter 4 –- Marty Delorenzo

To claim that Marty Delorenzo could kick the crap out of all of us at the same time was probably an exaggeration, but maybe not far from the truth. At six foot three and 240 pounds of solid muscle, he was definitely a force to be reckoned with. The good news was that even though he could snap your spine like a twig, he was a devoted pothead, and a gentle giant. He was also a loyal friend and considered me the leader of our group. The five of us had been friends since the third grade. For some reason, Marty always looked up to me and saw it as his duty to protect me at all costs. Thank God for that.

On most occasions Marty would ride with me and Petey, or with the guys, but according to him, he had a little business to take care of before we left, so he was going to meet us in Ellenville. He said not to wait for him at the Hotshops, because he wasn't sure what time he would be done with business. Did he actually say he had to take care of *business*? Now that was funny. First of all, Marty Delorenzo was not exactly the sharpest tool in the shed, and secondly, we all knew that by taking care of business, he was actually talking about scoring some pot in Newark. Although most of the time Marty could get his weed right at school, once in a while there would be a dry spell, and then he would have to buy his reefer from the black kids in Newark. I am not sure why, but those black kids always had grass, no matter what was happening in Woodbridge.

So, he would pack up his car, go get his drugs, and meet us at our New York State rendezvous spot. His vehicle was a cream colored, beat up '66 Pontiac Tempest. A car speaks volumes about the person who owns it and in Marty's case it was no different. The car was technically cream colored, but to be perfectly honest, it was *rust* and cream colored, with the emphasis on *rust.* The old radio had stopped working weeks ago, because he used to turn it on and off by pounding it with his fist. So he just bought a new FM/cassette player for the car, which just sat on the front bench seat, and the speakers were just laying in the back seat because he was too lazy to install any of it. Typical Marty. He would probably pop in one of his favorite bands, *Commander Cody and His Lost Planet Airmen*, and listen to "Seeds And Stems Again Blues" or their big hit "Hot Rod Lincoln," as he headed to our campsite. God bless that boy.

Chapter 5 — The Wagon Train (A Recap)

A wagon train usually involves a bunch of vehicles in a single file going to a single destination. Well, that is not exactly what we had going on, but it's close. Just to straighten things out and to keep them simple, here is a brief recap. First, my girlfriend Petey and I were in one car. Next, Joe Pensipine, Jimmy Waters, Johnny Miller, and Kellen O'Grady were in another car. Then Marty Delorenzo was in a third car. And finally there was "I don't know who the hell" in a fourth car, also heading to our camping destination in Ellenville, New York. The only thing I can tell you about the person in the fourth "mystery" car is, it was probably the same person who was hiding behind the bathroom door back at my apartment when I was leaving this morning.

Okay, now that you are all up to speed, we can proceed to the next chapter.

Chapter 6 -- Ellenville

Ellenville is considered a village, which is way cooler than a town. It is located in a valley surrounded by the Shawangunk Mountain range of the Catskill Mountains. Our campsite was about twenty minutes outside the village of Ellenville. My parents owned a beautiful piece of property located on the top of a mountain in an area known as Greenfield Park. I am not sure exactly how large the property was, but I am thinking around five or six acres. It really didn't matter, because for miles around in every direction it was surrounded by woods. There is a dirt road about two miles long that leads to the property. The front acre and a half is totally cleared and there is a lush green lawn loaded with clover and surrounded by gorgeous oaks, maples, and an assortment of conifers. Wildflowers dominate the field across the dirt road from my land, and just behind them, out of sight from the road, is a secluded little pond.

The pond, affectionately known as 'The Pond,' is amazingly beautiful. The water is a deep, tannic brown from the sap of the numerous white birch trees that surround its oval banks. What makes it such a special place, is that it is hidden from the world. Only a handful of people even know it exists. The pond is truly magical all year round, but in the fall, with the reflection of the red and yellow leaves on its mirror-like surface, it is so wonderful it almost takes your breath away.

Chapter 7 — My Plan

Okay, so my plan was to be the first one get to my property. After we left Hotshops, the other guys were going to stop in Ellenville to get some beer and supplies and then meet us. I knew Marty Delorenzo would be late; well, because he was always late. So I figured I would get to my property, leave all the shit in the car, grab a bag of marshmallows, a blanket, and Petey, and head over to the pond before everyone else arrived.

The day was perfect. It was mid July. The temperature must have been around eighty degrees with a gentle breeze rustling the treetops. The sky was a majestic blue, with white cotton ball clouds aimlessly drifting about. I could tell by looking at Petey that she was probably thinking the same thing as me, judging by the way she was looking at me with those sexy green eyes and beautiful smile. So, I grabbed the stuff, plus a little surprise I had for my girl, took her by the hand, and walked the footpath over to the pond. We didn't say a word to each other on the walk. When we got there I dropped the blanket and the marshmallows. Petey's arms found their way around my neck as her tongue found its way into my mouth. Our hands felt around all the familiar places until her hands got to my ass. She pulled back and asked, "What the heck have you got in your back pocket?"

I told her to step back, close her eyes and put out her hands. And you know what? She did. That's what I love about this girl. You ask her to do something so you can surprise her and she just does it. No questions asked and no complaining. All the other girls I had ever gone out with would always bust my balls when I would try to surprise them. For example, I would ask someone to close their eyes and she would want to know why, how come, what for, or just outright say "no." But not my sweet Petey; man, the girl was a gem. Ask her to step back and close her eyes, and she just did it. No argument, no ball busting; she just did it. What a breath of fresh air she was.

I reached into my back pocket and pulled out a miniature crystal vase with a petite red silk rose in it and placed it in her hands. When she opened her eyes, her lips drew back into an ear to ear smile, and I knew I had done good.

She was wearing a yellow tube top and tiny little blue jean cut-offs. She also had on cheap flip-flops and her toes were painted my favorite red. We embraced and kissed as I gently laid her down on the blanket. She was lying on her back and I went down by her feet to grab my bag of marshmallows. I slid her flip-flops off and softly kissed each one of her pretty toes. I then took a marshmallow out and started tracing the curves of her legs with the white puffy morsel. I followed the trail of the marshmallow with tender kisses all the way up to her inner thighs. I paused there for a moment and then slid my body tight alongside hers until my face was even with her breasts. Her eyes were closed and her breathing was getting deeper. I gingerly rolled down the yellow tube top and as each nipple was exposed it swelled to attention. I grabbed a new marshmallow and circled each nipple, followed by butterfly kisses. She was not the only one getting excited as I felt my own shorts getting uncomfortably tight. I kissed each nipple farewell as I guided my marshmallow along her neck and finally along her lips. Her tongue softly tasted and tested the sweetness and softness of puff and kiss. My hand found its way down to the top button of her shorts, and . . .okay, okay, that's enough of that. I mean this isn't a porno magazine for Christ's sake. This is an adventure story. If you want to get your rocks off, go get a *Hustler* magazine. Petey is my girl, and what we do is personal. Sorry.

But, continuing on with the tale. We were totally unaware of the maniacal eyes that were watching us only a few feet away in the bushes. I don't even want to think of what might have happened if at that very moment we didn't hear the unmistakable sound of Marty Delorenzo's beat up old Pontiac pulling onto my property a short distance away. Luckily our lovemaking had just ended and we were getting our clothes back on when we heard his car. At the same time, the maniac escaped as silently through the woods as he had come, and for the second time that day we had no idea of how fucking close we had come to being mutilated.

Chapter 8 — The Hillbillies

By hillbillies I don't mean Granny, Uncle Jed, and Ellie May, who, by the way, was one of the hottest chicks ever on TV. I am talking about real life, dyed-in-the-wool, in-bred, hillbillies. Ever since we were little kids spending our summer vacations up in Greenfield Park, we knew about the hillbillies. I mean, how could we not know? We used to pass their place every time we went to our property. The hillbillies were actually a family of about twelve people ranging in age from newborn to probably one hundred, who all lived in a broken down log cabin about three miles from our property. They had no electricity and no plumbing. No one was quite sure who was mother, father, sister, or brother. They probably all held more than one designation.

I mean, one of them could be both your sister and your wife, if you know what I mean. We rarely ever actually saw any of the hillbillies, but we knew they were there. There was always a skinny stream of smoke coming out of the little metal chimney on the roof of the shack, even in the summer, every time we passed. Although there were about twelve of them, the only one who had a name that anyone knew was Harold. Harold was a creepy ass dude right out of the movie *Deliverance*. My guess was he was about twenty years old. He was about six foot three, long and lean. He always sported a crew cut, and that, along with his six or seven teeth, made him a pretty menacing character of legendary status.

One time I actually came face to face with Harold. In the summer of sixty-nine, we were sitting in our house in New Jersey, when the phone rang. It was the Ellenville police informing us that the mobile home we had on our property (which was sold years ago and is no longer there) had been broken into. So the next day my father took us all up there to see the damages, and found out that all the clothing and silverware that we had left there was missing. Anyway, the day after we got there I was in Ellenville with my family and we ran into Harold on the street. The amazing thing was, the bastard was wearing my old shoes that I had left in our mobile home the summer before. Obviously, he was the one who broke in, but when I was eleven years old, I was too afraid of him to tell anyone what I had seen. As a kid I heard many tales about the hillbillies and how campers and tourists would come to the area and never be seen or heard from again. Everyone always suspected the hillbillies, but there was never any proof. I think even the local police were afraid of them.

Chapter 9– So Who the Hell is this Friggin' Maniac…. And Why is He Following Us?

Great question. If you recall, about a year ago, when I experienced an adventure detailed in "Blood on the High Seas" you may remember how my buddies and I were on a fishing party boat called *The Summer Wind*, which sailed out of Point Pleasant New Jersey. And you may also recall how there was this madman stowaway named John Paul Jones (not related to the famous guy who invented the Navy or the drummer of *Led Zeppelin*) who intended to kill everyone on board. But things backfired when an equally disturbed captain of said ship, Captain Terwilliger, turned the tables on John Paul and blew Jones' brains out. Then it got even more bizarre when Captain Terwilliger flipped out of his gourd and decided to try and kill the rest of us on his boat. Well, in the end my buddies and I got very lucky and managed to kill crazy Captain T before he killed us.

In any event, the fact is we killed the bastard. It was in all the papers and all the local TV news programs also covered the story. So, as it turns out, good ol' Captain T had a brother, named Bradley B. Terwilliger, who was just as fucked up as he was, and when he heard about us on the news, he swore he would never give up until each member of our gang was dead.

So that's who this friggin' maniac is.

Chapter 10 -– Fuckin-Ay

Petey and I had left the pond and were just approaching Marty Delorenzo's rust bucket car, which was parked on the clover lawn of my property, when we heard the rest of our gang's autos coming towards us from a distance. We turned around and could see a cloud of dust as the tires on their cars spun down the old dirt road.

"Fuckin-ay!" shouted Marty as he leaned out of his car window. Little did we all know that that phrase, "Fuckin-ay," would be a catch phrase the next year after the smash hit movie, *The Deer Hunter*, made it famous.

Not thirty seconds later the boys pulled up next to Marty's car and hopped out. Everyone exchanged greetings, and we all proceeded to un-pack our gear. The normal good-natured bullshit was thrown around and in no time our campsite was set up. It was quite a sophisticated little layout actually. There were four tents. One for Petey and me, one for Waters and Miller, one for Kellen O'Grady and Marty Delorenzo, and one for all of our gear.

There was a well on my property, which my parents had dug many years ago, which still had an operational spigot. We used that for our water. We brought out three folding card tables and a bunch of lawn chairs. The centerpiece of our campsite was an old stone grill, which my father and I had built years ago, but had stood up to the elements and the test of time. The only thing that made our adventure truly "roughing it," was the fact that there was no bathroom. For that you just found a tree to lean against to take care of your business.

Speaking of taking care of business, Kellen needed to relieve himself so he found what he thought was a private spot. What he didn't realize was that Marty had snuck up behind him and was about to poke him in the ass with a stick. "What the fuck!" Kellen screamed as he felt the stick poking his ass. He jumped and twisted and pissed all over his pant leg. Delorenzo dropped the stick and fell on the ground laughing.

"What the hell is the big idea ya big monkey?" yelled a red faced O'Grady at his huge friend rolling on the ground laughing.

"Sorry man," was all Marty could manage. He was laughing so hard we all thought he might actually piss himself too.

. . .

TIME OUT FROM OUR ADVENTURE!!!

Sorry, this has nothing to do with our story, but did you ever hear the song "Son of a Preacher Man" by Dusty Springfield? Man is that a great friggin' song. If you want to stop reading for a minute, and go look it up on Youtube, I give you permission. Wow, what a soulful song.

Anyway, back to our story.

Chapter 11 --- Petey!!

Life was good. There were burgers and hotdogs cooking on our grill. Good friends, beer, pot for Marty, and as Carl Sagan would say, "Billions and billions" of stars lit up the sky. I don't know about you, but for me, there is something magical about cooking on an open flame on a cool summer eve, with good friends, a mild buzz, and tons of stars in the sky.

Joe was doing the barbecuing and the rest of us were just shooting the shit and loving life. I was munching on a perfectly cooked burger and nursing a cool Bud and was in a heavy conversation with Marty, who was waxing philosophic on some bullshit topics like karma and fate. After awhile Jimmy Waters comes up to me and asks me if I knew where Petey was. I realized I was so into my conversation with Marty, I didn't even notice she was missing. Joe Pensipine heard Waters' question and yelled back that Petey told him that Mother Nature was calling and that she would be right back. I asked Joe how long ago that was and he replied about fifteen minutes earlier. I put down my burger and beer. I wasn't overly concerned, but I was a bit uneasy just the same. Maybe she had to do more than just "tinkle" as she liked to put it. I did not want to intrude on her privacy, but I was somewhat anxious. I figured I would give her five more minutes before I would actually start looking for her.

I took another bite of my burger, a sip of my Bud, and looked at Marty who was rambling on like a freight train about the existence of the universe. I decided enough time had passed, and determined to make sure everything was okay, I called out "Peeeeteeeey?" No reply. Again, "Pete!" I yelled. Again, no response. Everyone stopped their conversations and whatever they were doing and looked at me. I looked back, hunched my shoulders, and let out with a really loud, "PETEY!!" Nothing -- dead silence. Except for the crackling of the fire and the rustling of the leaves, I might as well have been deaf. Dead silence.

So Joe says, "Ya think you ought to go look for her?"

I think for a second and reply, "Yes."

All of my friends chime in at the same time that they will help me look, to which I respond, "No." It has only been a few minutes; there isn't much that could go wrong, and maybe Petey

really had to just "go."

I took one more gulp of my Bud, grabbed a flashlight, and

headed in the general direction Joe had said he had seen Petey

heading. I pointed the beam of the light erratically in front of me as

I walked. Nothing. I kept walking. "Petey!" I yelled, "If you're out

here, please answer me!" Silence. Wind and crickets were all I

heard. I kept walking in the dark with my beam of light in front of

me. Then, all of a sudden I stopped dead in my tracks. About twenty

yards ahead of me, in the beam from my flash light, I spotted

something white, nailed to a tree. I swear to God my heart skipped

a beat. My pace and heartbeat doubled. I got to the note and tore

it off the tree. I held the paper in my hand and pointed the white

ray of light at the note, which read: I have your whore. I can't wait

to enjoy her. Fuck you, and fuck your friends, come find me, but it

will be too late.

"Holly fuck shit!" I fell to my knees. The world started to

spin. I felt my burger and beer working their way back up the way they came in. They were dying to get out of me. I took my flashlight and whacked it into my head. Nothing. I did not even feel it. I whacked myself again and again, but still nothing. I was numb. Finally, I felt one of Mike Delorenzo's big paws grab my shoulder.

"What's up Chuck?" he asked. I couldn't even talk. I just handed him the note and sat silently as he read it. "Mother fucker!" he said. Not quite a yell, but you could tell it was coming. Again, "Mother fucker!" this time with a little more conviction. And finally, "Mother mother, mother FUCKER! I am going to kill this fucking piece of shit!" exclaimed Marty.

Just then, Jimmy Waters and Johnny Miller showed up. "What's up?" asked a confused Waters. Miller never said much, but you could tell by the look on his face that he was wondering the same thing. I looked at their wanting faces, not knowing what to say or think. I finally just blurted out, "Someone took Petey."

Chapter 12 -- Tinkle Tinkle Little Star...

Petey had just finished eating her well-done hot dog, smothered with ketchup and spicy brown mustard, just the way she liked it. She washed down the last bite by polishing off her second beer. She tossed her paper plate, napkin, and empty bottle into the black plastic hefty trash bag, which was on the ground next to Delorenzo's car. Then she grabbed a roll of toilet paper from the open trunk. She noticed that the guys were all busy yakking with each other, or stuffing their faces, and thought this would be a perfect time for her to slip off and take care of business. She had only walked about thirty yards into the woods before she spotted a perfect dead tree to balance herself on. Petey undid her jeans and slid them down to her knees. It was pretty dark, but she wasn't really afraid. She was a bit apprehensive, though. *There could be a bear or something lurking around out there, couldn't there?* she thought.

She was also thinking about the time she and Chuck were driving to see a *Who* concert at Madison Square Garden. On the way there she had to tinkle like a madwoman, so she made Chuck pull over. She got out and stooped down behind the car door to do

her thing. She got back in the car, went to the concert and had a

hell of a great time. It wasn't until the next morning that Petey

realized that she had poison ivy everywhere. It was one of the most

embarrassing times of her life. That was what she was thinking

about when she felt a strong hard hand come from behind her and

grab her mouth shut so she couldn't scream. The other hand went

around her throat and lifted her to her feet. It happened so fast, she

forgot to stop peeing, and most of the warm liquid sprayed all over

her abductor's legs. Both her attacker's and Petey's adrenalin were

pumping, so neither of them even noticed.   Without releasing his

hand from her mouth, his other hand disappeared momentarily

only to return to her neck an instant later, this time with a six-inch

razor sharp knife in it. He motioned for her to start walking, and

without even thinking, she pulled her jeans up and buttoned them.

The two started to blend into one dark shadow as they went deeper

and deeper into the woods. At one point, the only thing visible was the white toilet paper hitching a ride on the well-worn heel of the kidnapper's right boot.

Chapter 13 -- Harold the Hillbilly is About to Die!

All the guys were practically falling over themselves just trying to keep out of each other's way. No one knew exactly what to do, but they were so jazzed up, they couldn't sit still. Except for me. I hadn't moved an inch in five minutes. I just crouched where I was, closed my eyes, and tried to make sense of what was going on. Then all of a sudden, I stood up, opened my eyes and said one word, "Harold."

Everyone stopped dead in their tracks. Joe walked over to me, put a hand on my shoulder and asked, "What did you say"?

"Harold," I said again.

Everyone gathered closer. They looked at me like I was some voodoo witchdoctor about to sprout some magical chanting that would bring the long awaited rains so that our plants would grow.

Delorenzo was the first to speak. "Huh?" was all he could get out.

Then Joe Pensipine asked, "What do you mean, 'Harold,' Chuck?"

"I mean we are miles and miles from anywhere and the only people on this mountain are us and the Hillbillies. I don't know why, but for some reason, I think Harold the Hillbilly took Petey. It has to be him. No one else even knows we are here. He must have heard our cars when we came up here, and he must have been watching us from the woods. I know where he lives, and tonight, Harold the Hillbilly is going to die."

"I can think of a reason he took her," said an excited Kellen O'Grady. "I bet he is going to bring her back to his shack, throw her on the bed, tie her t...", Whap! Marty Delorenzo's huge hand smacked the back of his chubby friend's head.

"Shut the hell up!" yelled Delorenzo.

"No, you shut the hell up!" retorted Kellen.

"Both of you shut the fuck up!" directed a stern, yet controlled, Pensipine. Then he added, "Chuck, tell us what you need us to do and we'll do it. You name it, and consider it done."

"Fine," I said. "As fast as possible, everyone grab anything that even remotely resembles a weapon. We have no idea how many hillbillies are actually still living in the shack with Harold, and we will need all the help we can get to make this an even playing field. I'm not sure of what kind of arsenal they'll have, but I'm positive that at minimum they will have shotguns. We will only have the element of surprise and whatever we find in the next couple of minutes."

My friends and I scurried about like young children on an LSD Easter Egg Hunt. Six minutes later we were all back together except for Kellen O'Grady, who was still scurrying.

Joe Pensipine brought a hatchet. Johnny Miller had a baseball and a horseshoe. Jimmy Waters had a badminton racquet. Delorenzo had his six-foot fiberglass two-piece fishing pole. A number 7g Rapala lure, complete with two sets of treble hooks was attached to the end of the line. I think I was in shock. I didn't know if I wanted to laugh or cry.

I found my beautiful leather sheathed hunting knife, which my sweet Petey had given me as an anniversary present at the start of this trip.

"Okay, let's move out" I said.

Miller asked, "Are we going to drive?"

"No John," I answered. "Element of surprise."

As we headed on foot into the dark woods, none of us realized Kellen O'Grady wasn't with us. Quietly, and without speaking, we made our way through the hardwood forest. The moon was full on this crystal clear night in July. Our eyes adjusted quickly to the night's darkness. Fifteen minutes later, in the distance we could see a light in the window of Harold the Hillbilly's shack. We huddled up and hid behind two huge boulders at the edge of the Hillbilly property.

We had a pretty good vantage point and could scope out the situation pretty well from where we hid. We were about twenty-five yards from the careworn, wooden back door of the shack. The Hillbilly house was very small and shaped like a monopoly house, except the shack was brown, not green. As I looked through the window of the back door, I could see right across the tiny house to the front door. I could tell someone was in there because I could see the top of someone's head. It looked like a crew cut. I could not see what he was doing, but I could see what appeared to be several sharp and pointy rods leaning against the wall on the far side of the room. My mind started racing when I heard Pensipine whisper "Looks like he has a fire going on the right side of the house."

I shifted my eyes to the right side of the house and could see the flickering light cast from what was probably a small fire in some sort of pit. Why would Harold the Hillbilly be burning a fire on such a hot summer night? I could picture the crazy bastard heating the rods in the fire and then torturing my sweet Petey with them. We had to act fast. I prayed I was wrong, and I prayed I was in time to save Petey.

"Jimmy, you and Miller circle around the left side of the house and stand by the front door. When you get there, take Millers baseball and hit it high in the air over the roof so Joe, Delorenzo and I can see it. As soon as we see it, we will count to five and storm the back door. At the same time, you two crash in the front door. I don't know what to expect, but I know we have to move fast and save my girl. Any questions? No? Good. And guys, be careful."

Without saying a word, Jimmy Waters and Johnny Miller took off. It was under a minute, but seemed like an eternity, when we saw the baseball come flying over the roof of the shack. The three of us counted to five in our heads, ran pell-mell to the back door and crashed it in. Harold the Hillbilly just about had a stroke. He fell off his chair and landed face down on the wooden kitchen floor with his hands crisscrossed over the back of his head. "What the hell?" he must have been thinking, when he looked up and saw me standing over him holding my knife, Pensipine with an ax and Delorenzo with a fishing pole.

"Now wait awhile, wait awhile," pleaded a very confused Harold. "My Gran Pappy always would tell me, "Boy, even you and a blind nigger don't even know when the sun is shinin'." We looked at each other, confused, and then back at the Hillbilly lying on the floor.

Harold continued, "He would tell me that sayin' all my life, but I never know'd what he was talkin' about. I *still* don't know, but for the first time in my life, I think this is a sityation what fits. What 'n hell is goin' on here?"

Marty Delorenzo turned to Pensipine and asked, "Even a blind *what,* don't even know *what?*"

"I'm not sure, but I think he said even you and a blind nigger don't even know when the sun is shining." They both shrugged their shoulders then turned to me. I was trying to get a fix on the "sityation." I had three thoughts in my mind. First, I could see that Harold the Hillbilly was lying on the floor, but only a few feet away was a shotgun leaning on the table where he was sitting before we crashed in, uninvited. Second, I thought, "W*here the hell was Petey, and what did this bastard do to her?*" And third, I realized that Johnny Miller and Jimmy Waters never came crashing into the house via the front door. Where the hell were they? For that matter, where the heck was Kellen O'Grady, and when did he disappear?

With many unanswered questions running through my mind, the first thing I did was grab the shotgun from out of the reach of Harold the Hillbilly.

"Now wait awhile; wait awhile," Harold said as he sat up on his haunches on the hard uncarpeted floor. "Take it easy with that 'ol girl, she's likely to go offn' by accident ifn' you don't handle her right" he said, never taking his eyes off of me.

"Don't worry about me, I've handled shotguns before. You better start worrying about yourself and what's going to happen to you if you hurt one hair on Petey's head."

"Now wait awhile; wait awhile. Who is Petey? Ain't no one here but me."

I walked across the minuscule kitchen and poked my head in the only other room in the house. It was also a miniature sized room, a bedroom, but surprisingly neat and clean, as was the kitchen we were all in. It was apparent that Petey was never here. Everything was in its place and there was no sign of any struggle. As I turned back to the kitchen, to my horror, Harold was lunging towards

Pensipine. In a flash he managed to grab the ax from Joe's hand and maneuver his body so he was standing behind Pensipine with his one hand holding Joe's arm behind his back, and his other hand holding the cold steel blade of the ax to my best friend's throat.

Chapter 14 -- Meanwhile, Back at the Farm.

About a half mile through the woods sat a small, rugged, weathered, primitive handmade hunting shack. The one large window at the left end of the shack was filthy, but you could see there was the glow of a kerosene hurricane lamp radiating from within. I knew this place well from all the summers I had spent vacationing on our property, which was not very far from the shack. It was built by hunters many, many years ago, and every fall someone who knew someone who knew the original occupants of the shack would occupy the place for a week to ten days and hunt everything from rabbits and squirrels in the small game season to beautiful white tail deer and bears, in the big game seasons.

It was a tradition that whoever went to the shack one year, would bring enough canned and preserved foods for the occupants the following year. It was really quite cool. There would always be a surprise awaiting you when you arrived. It would always be something special too. Because legend had it, the better food you provided your fellow hunters, the more the hunting gods would be kind to you.

Inside the rickety door were two identical rooms. Might as well call them *all purpose* rooms, seeing as one could do whatever one wanted in either of the two rooms. Well, that might have been true on hunting trips. Tonight however, four of my best friends were hogtied and not free to do whatever they wanted inside this shack. They all had their hands and feet tied together and their mouths were stuffed with rags. Jimmy Waters and Johnny Miller were bound in the sitting position and were placed in opposite corners of the room on the south end of the shack. Kellen O'Grady was lying on the floor on his back, with his hands tied together resting on his swollen belly. Petey was hogtied in the traditional fashion, with her hands and feet bound together behind her back, just at her butt. She was the only one not on the floor. She was on her stomach on the only table in the shack. Around the table were six wooden chairs, which were now scattered about from the commotion when Petey was getting tied up.

Walking back and forth, randomly, but in some sort of preordained geometric design was Bradley B. Terwilliger. As he approached each of his bound victims, he kept repeating, over and over again, in a multitude of ways, his name. Each time the five foot four inch little man put more emphasis on different parts of his name. And though the twerp started out speaking almost in a whisper, he eventually ended up shouting.

"Brad *Terwilliger*, *Bradford* B. Terwilliger, Bradley *Barton* Terwilliger, *Bradford* Barton Terwilliger, *B, B, T,*" and finally, "Brad, The *King* of all *fucking B's* **Terrrwilliger!"**

Needless to say, the ranting of the dwarf-sized madman had my compadres almost crapping their pants. All of them but one, anyway. The calmest of the captive quartet, by far, was Petey. She was busy thinking that perhaps Brad Terwilliger might be the hairiest human being she had ever seen. His hair was reddish brown and frizzy, almost the texture of an old Brillo pad after all the soap had been used up and what remained of it sitting on the sink was starting to rust. It was piled high on his head and was gathered together by a rubber band just below the nape of his neck. His ears were the worst part. Petey imagined that at almost any moment small barn animals would come rushing out of the bushes growing on his ears. He had the kind of beard that would make you want to scream, "Trim that fucking thing, would you please!" It wasn't very bushy, but it started way too high on his cheeks and ran too far down his alligator sun burnt neck. This grey, brown, and reddish mess was greeted by long, bushy silver hairs peeking out from the top of his purple wife-beater tee. Bright red shorts covered too little of his forested legs, which were rooted in his white socks and white sneakers.

"*Yes*" Petey thought, "*I have been kidnapped by a dwarf werewolf, with absolutely no taste for fashion.*" This peculiar thought almost got her killed on the spot. Between her panic and this bizarre thought, her nerves took over, and though she was gagged, she started laughing. Brad heard her muffled yelps and came to investigate what was its source. When he realized that she was laughing, red shards of pain ignited inside his brain. "*How dare this bitch be laughing,*" he thought, when the reaction he craved was to see fear take over her entire body. He wanted to see her eyeballs straining to escape the warmth and comfort of their resting place inside their sockets. He wanted to see greenish blue veins poking at her neck so that the lava from her wildly beating heart could navigate its way around her body.

He ached to see tiny droplets of salty sweat forming on her brow, above her beautiful green eyes. He suddenly realized that thinking like this was causing him to grow a little stiff in the shorts. He grabbed Petey's hair and yanked her head back. Unexpectedly, a smile broke through the madness of his face. It was an evil smile just the same, a smile with no kindness to support it. He looked deep into her eyes and said in a gruff, gravelly voice,"So, are you enjoying yourself? Glad to see you're having a pleasant time. Comfy? Anything I can get for you, sweetie?" And then he added, "What's that? You enjoy laughing so much you want me to tickle you?" as if he were responding to something she said to him. Then he continued, "Oh, I see, you want me to tickle your pointy little nipples, and then maybe do a little diddling in your hot little playground?"

Petey glanced down and noticed his little dickens was straining the material of his shorts. She thought to herself, "*I wonder if dog boy's penis has a red tip on it like a dog?*" and again the laughter gurgled out of her against her will. Her laughing had a deflating effect on his ding dong, and instantly, his thoughts changed from torturing and fucking her, to killing her. "*Fuck her, who the hell was she? She didn't deserve the pleasure of being pounded by his jackhammer.*" And he would have snapped her neck that second, but an even deeper desire overtook him. He wanted to watch the expression on el fuckito, Chuck Kikel's, face, when he, Brad, the king of all fucking B's, killed all six of his friends one by one. Brad could picture it in his demented mind. Kikel would have to beg for mercy, until he was ready to puke, for each one of his friends' lives. He would beg and plead, and then BBT would slowly but surely kill them all until not one of those sorry assholes who killed his brother was left alive.

Okay, so somehow, mean old miserable Brad, managed to round up his herd of kidnapees and get them all onto their feet. They were all similarly bound, hands together behind their backs and gags in their mouths. He also removed the shoes of his prisoners, so if they tried to run, their feet would hurt too much to get any distance away. By the way, I am not even going to tell you what Bradford B did when he took off Petey's shoes. I mean nobody wants to hear how Brad sniffed and licked the poor girl's toes. Nah, I didn't think so.

So the merry band traipsed off into the black forest to meet a fate none of them would ever forget.

Chapter 15 -- Now, Wait Awhile; Wait Awhile.

"Now, wait awhile; wait awhile" said Harold the Hillbilly. He was talking directly into my eyes. Even though we were locked eye to eye, like two tomcats staring each other down in a dark moonlit alleyway, we also were both utilizing our peripheral vision to its optimum effect. Mine was focused in on the ax blade against Pensipine's throat, and Harold's line of sight was zoomed in on his shotgun in my hand. It was as if I could read his thoughts. He was wondering, *"Did I leave any shells in that shotgun"*? And to tell you the truth, I was wondering the same thing myself.

"Put down the ax and let Joe go," I said in a low and steady voice. I continued, "I am a pretty good shot and you don't want me to have to prove that," I said.

"Now, wait awhile; wait awhile, I don't think you're gonna' shoot me," said Harold. "And for many a reason. Firstly, I don't think there are any shells in that there pea shooter, an iff'n that there was, I don't think you *really* wanna', bein' as you're city folk an' you don't barely know me and I ain't done nutthin' to hurt nobody, not even your friend. And you know whatever else is up, I will hep ya' get your friend back."

"Okay, cards on the table time," I thought to myself. "Am I to believe the terrible, horrible, tourist killing, legendary, Harold the Hillbilly, was offering a hand to a stranger in need? A stranger who not only broke into his home a few moments ago, but was also holding his own shotgun on him.

I lowered the shotgun just a few inches and asked, "What's your game Harold? What did you do with my girlfriend, Petey? What is with the fire and the sharp metal spikes in the corner? If you don't have Petey, then what are those things for? Well?"

Harold let down his ax and Joe seized the opportunity to elbow the big boy in the stomach. Air flew out of Harold's lungs and he doubled over. Joe sunk and spun, and in a second was standing next to me.

"Shoot him, shooot him!" Pensipine pleaded. But I was watching Harold closely. At first I thought he was crying, or trying to get his wind back, but then I realized he was laughing.

"What the hell are you laughing at?" I asked. Harold, slowly composing himself, said in a sentence that was interspersed with staccato breaks, so he could regain his composure and stop laughing so hard, answered, "I bet, *breath – breath,* that I, *long breath*, am going to be the first person to be shot for toasting marshmellers."

"*Huh? What*?" were just two of the questions going through both my head and Joe's. Another question was, "*Okay, If Harold the Hillbilly didn't have Petey, where the hell was she?*"

"What did you say?" I asked Harold. Now standing erect again, and breathing more normally, Harold answered, "I said, you two boys are about to assassinate a guy for toasting marshmellers." Harold twisted his head around and pointed with his eyes toward the counter behind him. We followed his glance and suddenly

noticed there were five bags of marshmallows on the counter. Four

were factory sealed, and one was torn open with a few mallows

obviously missing.

"Marshmallows? *Marshmallows!* Is that what you are up to,

toasting marshmallows? That's what the metal spikes are for?"

Marty Delorenzo asked rhetorically.

"Uh huh," answered Harold the H, disregarding the

rhetorical nature of Delorenzo's question..

"Yessiree Bob," continued Harold. "Ya see, my family is all

offn' Kerhonkson sellin' sweet corn on the side of route forty-two.

And me, well I was plannin' on treatin' myself to some toasty

marshmellers."

Joe, Marty and I looked at each other. "Marshmellers!

Marshmellers! You can never have enough good marshmellers

around is what I always say," said Pensipine, as all four of us finally

started relaxing.

"Now even me and a blind..."

"Woa," my two friends and I interrupted. "Harold, you must stop saying that terrible saying, it's just not right," I said, probably echoing the thoughts of both Joe and Marty.

"Now wait awhile; wait awhile, I never meant nuthin' bad by it. In fact, I don't even know what the hell it means. It just sumpin' my gran' pappy used to say all the time is all. Now can one of you boys tell me what the hell is goin' on here?" asked Harold, calmly, yet firmly.

So I gave him the *Reader's Digest* version of what had happened, and Harold the Hillbilly said he thought he could help us. He told us how he *knewd* these woods like the back of his hand, and he was suspicious of someone *messin'* around up at the old huntin' lodge. "Huntin' lodge," that killed me. It's amazing how different people view different things or situations. I guess that's what makes the world go around. I guess if everyone saw things the same way, there would be no use for lawyers. Was there ever a need for lawyers? Man, do I hate lawyers. But, I am starting to digress*

Harold's plan was for Marty to put down the fishing rod, or pole, as Harold called it, and all of us should instead take a metal spike as a weapon. We would sneak up on the lodge, and between his shotgun, my knife and the spikes, we should have enough fire power to capture the son of a bastard kidnapper.

All of us did as Harold suggested and gathered our spikes and started out the door of the cabin. All of us except Marty Delorenzo, who was probably feeling the effects of the munchies gnawing at him, and grabbed two big paws full of marshmallows and slid them down the metal spikes with the stealth and grace of a surgeon suturing the left aorta ventricle after completing an extremely delicate bypass surgery.

As we walked past the huge fire Harold had previously built, Delorenzo couldn't resist the urge to stop and toast his marshmallows in the big flame.

"Are you kidding me?" asked an amazed Joe Pensipine. "You actually think we have time to stand here and toast marshmallows, when Petey's, Kellen's, Waters' and Miller's lives could all be in jeopardy?"

My ears heard this, but my mind did not fully register what was going on until I turned and saw the big gorilla standing there with a four foot metal spike with four marshmallows kabobbed on one end, toasting them in the fire. In a second I was standing next to Marty and before he knew what hit him, I had snatched the marshmallow kabob from him.

* Usually, when I am writing a story, I like to use the word *anyway* to steer my readers in a new direction or to get back on track when I start wandering. My friend Lauren was reading a passage from this story when she suggested I use *I digress*, instead of *anyway*, so, to make her happy, I added, "I am starting to digress" above. Sorry for the digression. CK

Chapter 16 -- Fire in the Hole

Crickets. The only sound you could hear in the hot still night was crickets. I'd like to say you could hear an occasional great horned owl, but I would be lying. But I would still like to say it.

As they headed out into the forest, the sound of tiny twigs snapping under the pressure of their bare feet was the only sound added to the symphony being played by the crickets. Kellen O'Grady was on point. The rest followed in single file: Miller, Waters, Petey, and finally, Bradford T., bringing up the rear.

I am not sure what Kellen O'Grady was thinking when he suddenly started running, but if he was thinking, "*If I run, that nutjob will kill me,*" he would have been pretty damn close to the truth. With his heart beating madly at his chest, jelly belly O'Grady took a bad step into a gopher hole as he tried to make a break. The enormous pressure from his massive bulk onto his awkwardly bent ankle, snapped the joint connecting his foot to his leg. Hot streams of pain raced up the rotund ones leg and didn't stop until they collided with his brain. His mammoth body fell to the ground in a colossal heap of sweaty blubber. By the time his head hit the ground he had already passed out from the pain. From a distance

he resembled a pile of dirty laundry. His friends instinctively started

to run to aid their fallen comrade, but Brad Terwilliger had other

thoughts in his head. With the quickness of a man half his age, he

blindsided the remaining trio of detainees and laid them face down,

side by side, on the ground. For the first time since they were

captured, Petey's terror equaled that of her friends.

Without breaking stride, Bradley was suddenly hovering

over Kellen's defeated body. As he reached around to the rear

waistband of his pants, Brad pulled out a knife. He thought he was

only thinking in his head, but the words actually left his lips in a low

growly voice. "So long fatboy. Sorry it had to end like this, ya' know.

I would have liked to bring you back to the cabin to torture you to

death in front of Mr. Kikel. Oh well, I guess this will just have to do.

Bye-bye fat ass." With that, he raised the blade high in the air and

slammed it down into poor Kellen O'Grady's lower back. Brad had

been aiming higher, trying to puncture a lung, but he was just as

happy with his new target. He figured he would either hit a kidney, spleen, or pancreas, and the piece of shit would slowly bleed to death.

For the first time since her abduction, the sound that escaped Petey's lips was not nervous laughter, but a terrifying scream, albeit a scream muffled by a gag. The truth be told, Waters and Miller were adding their own anguished, but still muffled, screams of horror.

Chapter 17 -- The End

Well dear readers, that's where this story ends. After all, it's the journey, not the ending, which makes a story interesting. I leave the end up to you. Okay, Okay, Okay! Just kidding. I was just thinking how pissed off I was at one of my favorite authors, Mr. Stephen King, when after years of reading his *Dark Towers* series of seven books, he pulled exactly that stunt. He told me, the reader, to finish the ending myself. With all due respect, Mr. King, "GO FUCK YOURSELF!" We had a deal: you write and I read; it's that simple. Nowhere did I agree that you write and I read *and* write.

I know, once again, I digress. So, without further ado, sit back and relax and enjoy the rest of my tale.

Chapter 17 -- The Real End

With sheer terror in their eyes, the remaining captives looked back at their slowly dying friend Kellen O'Grady as they distanced themselves from him at Terwilliger's beckoning.

"Oh, don't you worry about him, the fat turd will probably pass out from the pain before he actually dies," were the words that broke the silence minutes later.

Bradley Terwilliger had led the trio to an open pocket of grass along the trail they had been walking along. From where they stood, they could clearly see Harold the Hillbilly, and his new entourage, through the trees. Because the night was stone silent but for the crickets, and because sound carries well in the mountain air, Brad could hear every word his conniving adversaries were saying. When he heard that they were moments away from coming after him, he decided that the best defense was a good offense. Once again he grabbed the knife from his waistband, and this time it was Petey's neck that the bloodied razor sharp steel blade threatened.

I was just about to bring the four marshmallows out of the fire when I suddenly saw my friends and their taskmaster emerging from the forest edge. It took a few seconds for what I was seeing to register. I was shocked to see that Harold's mind worked as quickly as mine.

"Now wait awhile; wait awhile," he started as he moved his shotgun with the stealth of a navy seal sniper. "Let her go or I'll shoot you" finished a very menacing sounding Harold.

I guess that Bradley wasn't as intimidated by his voice as I was because he just chuckled and said, "Anyone can see that that is a shotgun you got there, and there is a better than fifty-fifty chance that you'll hit this little girly here by mistake. So, why don't you just put that shotgun down and maybe I won't kill you. The rest of these scumbags are going to die one by one so that Mr. Chucky Kikel over there can witness their demise. Then I'll kill him and my revenge will be complete as equal payment for killing my brother Cappy T on his beloved boat, *The Summer Wind*."

I wondered what Harold would do. And without hesitation he gave me my answer. "One thing you ain't understandin' mister bowie knife, is that I don't give a crap if'n I hits her or not. I don't even know this dizzy dame or care if she lives or dies. Her crazy ass friends broke into my house and I'm not concerned whether they live or die either. So here is what I propose: you let me have them to do whatever the hell I wants to do with them by myself. I'm thinking you probably tapped into that pretty filly by now, and I wouldn't mind doin' it to her once or twice myself before I dispose of her and her peckerwood friends."

"Nice try Jed Clampett, but I ain't buying your garbage" said a crazed Bradley Terwilliger. I think you ain't got the balls to try to speak to me like that and actually follow through. I do believe you are a sheep in a lion's clothing. So I think you better put down your weapon before you get yourself killed," barked Bradley.

Time froze. For some reason, the lyrics to the *Lovin'*

Spoonful song that went *"Did you ever have to make up your mind,*

Pick up on one and leave the other behind,

It's not often easy, and not often kind, did you ever have to make up

your mind?" kept running through my head. I knew the moment of

truth had come, and I had to make my move.

Now, I knew that Petey and my friends would understand

what the heck I meant if I yelled "Routine Six!" The guys would

know because when we were kids, we loved the old TV show, *The*

Bowery Boys, and each week when the gang of kids got into crazy

situations, the leader of the gang, Slip Mahoney would yell out a

random routine number like *routine nine*, when they got into a

terrible jam. Somehow, all the kids in the gang would understand

some pre-arranged plan they had practiced for just such an

occasion, and all of them would spring into action at once. Petey

would know what "routine six" meant because when I told her

about our adventure on the high seas during which we were faced

with another deadly situation with Bradley B. Terwilliger's brother,

Captain T, I shouted "routine six" and we all sprang into action.

Although my friends and I never actually planned any *routines*

whatsoever, we all knew it meant to take drastic action. So I was

pretty sure my friends would know what to do, but I had no idea

what Harold the Hillbilly would do. Would he panic and try to shoot

Brad and maybe kill Petey by mistake? Would he drop his weapon?

Or would he just freeze from fear and excitement and do nothing?

Who knew, but I had to take my chances, because it was now or

never, so I shouted, "Routine six!"

It all happened in a blink of an eye, but it also appeared to

happen in slow motion. The second I gave the command, Johnny

Miller, and Jimmy Waters started jumping up and down and

screaming through their gags. Joe Pensipine and Marty Delorenzo

started running in opposite directions. Harold picked up instantly on

what was happening and blasted two echoing shotgun blasts

directly into the night sky, and Petey elbowed Brad in the guts,

broke away from his grip and fell to the ground. In all the mass

confusion, poor Brad had no idea what was going on. It was all up to me, Chuck Kikel, to put an end to it right then and there. What happened next seems bizarre now, but at the time it seemed as natural as dunking an Oreo cookie into a glass of ice cold milk. I looked down at my hand and realized the four marshmallows on the end of my metal spike had caught on fire. I lifted the flaming morsels back behind my head and launched them as hard as I could at Terwilliger. The fireball of goo slid off the end of my metal stick and separated into two equal size fireballs which made direct hits on either side of Bradley B. Terwilliger's nose, completely covering his eyes and transforming his face into a weird surrealistic combination of a Salvador Dali, Pablo Picasso painting. He instinctively reached for his face, forgetting he had his Bowie knife in his hand, and proceeded to stab himself in the jugular. As he fell to the ground, the picture that remains in my mind's eye is that of a flaming banana split. My ice cream sundae foe lie squirming on the ground, gooey white and red flames smothering his head and shoulders. I believe it was Delorenzo who grabbed a burlap tarp and thankfully threw it over the horrific mess which used to be Brad's head.

Epilogue

Every year, on the anniversary of what is now referred to as "The toasting of Bradley B. Terwilliger," my girl Petey and I, along with my friends Joe Pensipine, Johnny Miller, Jimmy Waters, Marty Delorenzo, and Kellen O'Grady take a trip up to my property, on the outskirts of the village of Ellenville, and visit our good friend, Harold the Hillbilly. We always laugh and drink (and yes, Marty still gets high), and we all retell the story of what happened on that fateful weekend. We talk about how lucky we were to have meet Harold, and how it was a miracle that because the way Kellen had fallen and because of his huge girth, his own body weight had acted like a tourniquet and prevented him from bleeding to death.

Petey would always wear the anniversary present I finally gave her which was a fouteen karat gold necklace of a marshmallow on the end of a stick, which I had my friend who owned Ford's

Jewelers design for me. As our weekends would come to an end,

and we all said our goodbyes, someone would always start singing,

and everyone else would sing along, *"For he's a jolly good fellow,"*

to me.

So long for now, friends...

Chuck Kikel

West Rim

Chuck Kikel

Printed in the United States of America

First Printing, 2014

ISBN -9781503389106

Kid Kikel Productions Inc.
Tampa Florida

Dedicated to all my Wives .....this is all your fault

BOOK 3

WEST RIM

By Chuck Kikel

Introduction

Ah, my faithful readers, welcome home. It has been awhile since we talked. Many changes have taken place in my life, as I am sure have in yours as well. Some changes are small and barely noticeable, like your choices of TV shows or styles of music. Other changes may be huge and immediately noticeable, like graduating college or getting married. Maybe you have gone from going out with your friends on weekends and partying, to now being drunk before you make it to McDonalds' for your breakfast EggMcMuffin. Or maybe you have become a transvestite. Who knows?

Whatever, we are all friends here, and I judge none and love you all dearly.

As most of you know, for an average teenager from New Jersey, your old buddy Chuck has had some hair raising things happen to me in my youth. From the time the boys and I had to mutinize Captain Jules Terwilliger aboard the party boat *Summer Wind*, to the time we had to rescue my girlfriend Petey (with the assistance of Harold the Hillbilly) from the savage and disgusting hands of the hairy little dog boy named Bradford B Terwilliger (actually the brother of the aforementioned demented Captain, Jules Terwilliger).

Well, this next adventure takes place nearly two years after the demise of Bradford B Terwilliger. So sit back, get comfortable, and let me share with you the *Latest Wild Adventure of Chuck Kikel*, "West Rim."

Prelude 1
Brativa (BRAAT –i – VUH) Domotuski

In 1928, in a very small Russian village named Avenya, a homely baby girl named Brativa Domotuski was born. Her parents were Shethey and Svetlanka.

Svetlanka died while giving birth to Brativa, from a rare condition, known as amniotic fluid embolus, in which the amniotic fluid mysteriously gets into the circulation of the mother and basically fucks everything up. Typically there is heart failure, lung failure, bleeding from the nose, mouth and uterus (and that's the good stuff) to eventually, and thankfully, death.

Shethey, Brativa's father and a blacksmith by trade, was forced to raise the child all by himself. He was a hard man with a hard life and he expected much of the same for his daughter (Except she was a girl, so she would be a hard woman, not a hard man).

Prelude 2

In 1944, while the Allied Forces were busy invading Anzio Italy, a nineteen year old Marine private, Sean Terwilliger, was busy invading a sixteen year old Russian girl named Brativa Domotuski, whom he met in a GI bar while he was on leave. Eight months and two weeks later, 7lb 9oz Jules Terwilliger was born. The three somehow found their way to America, and ended up living in the Pine Barrens of New Jersey. A year later, and nearly starved to death, the Terwilligers moved to nearby Toms River, where Sean made enough money from his meager salary and tips working as a mate on the partyboat *The Sunking.* By the spring of that year, Brativa had another bun in the oven, and shortly thereafter she gave birth to Bradford B. Terwilliger.

Brativa loved her children, but hated their father. Her eldest son, Jules Terwilliger, was basically a good kid who loved when his daddy took him to work with him. Jules' father, Sean, knew his boss, the captain of *The Summer Wind*, was a very nice man and did not mind having young Jules aboard. After all, the boy loved helping the other mates do their jobs and the customers got a kick out of the lad.

Bradford B. Terwilliger, on the other hand, was a barn burner. If there was trouble to be had, you could bet your socks that ole B.B.T. had something to do with it, but no one could ever catch him. (I think T.S. Eliot must have known a kid like Bradford, and that is who he based his character Macavity on in his poems which eventually became the Broadway smash hit musical, *Cats.* Whenever I think about Brad Terwilliger, I hear the words from the song, "*Macavity, Macavity, there's no one like Macavity. He's broken every human law, he breaks the law of gravity --- For when*

they reach the scene of crime Macavity's not there!")

Anyway, the kid was trouble. But the love of a mother often turns a blind eye to the reality of what an asshole her son really is.

Yes, it's true that her husband Sean was a hard worker, but he was a hard cheater too, never passing up any opportunity that presented itself to him. But that is not why Brativa hated Sean; of course it was part of the reason, but more of the reason was how violent he became when drinking. Sean drank as much as the poor bluefish he gutted every day. When the booze started singing, Sean started swinging, and unfortunately, Brativa, more often than not, was the recipient of his fury. In fact, he hit her so hard once, that he knocked the front left tooth out of her mouth. He did feel a little bad about that, so to make it up to her, he had a gold plated false tooth put in the empty space. Now in those days there were no rap stars with grills, and Brativa looked totally stupid. But Brativa was a very tough woman and could care less about her gold tooth, because the only thing she really cared about was her two boys.

Not surprisingly, when her husband Sean died from accidently falling out of his bedroom window, Brativa did not seem too upset about it. The police thought she was a little on the cold side when she told them she was asleep when her drunken husband fell to his death, but they just thought the poor woman must have been in shock. (Yeah, right).

But enough of this preluding around, let's get to our story already.

> I knew a lady who came from Duluth
> Bitten by a dog with a rabid tooth
> She went to her grave just a little too soon
> Flew away howling on the yellow moon
>
> Where do bad folks go when they die
> They don't go to heaven where the angels fly
> Go to a lake of fire and fry
> See them again 'till the Fourth of July
> ■ Nirvana *Lake of Fire*

"Petey opened her eyes and her first thought was that Betty was dead. There was blood all over the left side of her face and she lay motionless. Then, after a few seconds, she noticed Betty's chest rising and falling and knew the woman wasn't dead after all. Before

she could let out a sigh of relief, she heard some disturbing sound coming from her left side, the direction where Chuck and Joe were standing next to Harold the Hillbilly, whose condition was rapidly deteriorating…………………………"

Chapter One

Holy Crap Chuck!

I just walked in the door to my apartment, when I heard my girlfriend Petey yelling, "Holy crap Chuck! Get over here quick, we're on TV."

Obviously I knew why we were on the six o'clock Eyewitness News, because earlier that morning, the camera crew and a reporter were knocking at my front door. I am not sure how they found out about what happened between Mrs. Planski and us, but I guess not too much that happened to Stash Planski's widow, didn't make the news these days. You see, Stash Planski, AKA Stash, "The King of all Polish Sausages," owner and creator of the billion dollar franchise, *Snausages* (famous not only for their 12 different sausage dishes on the menu, but for their world class, melt in your mouth homemade pierogies) was one of the most generous people in the Tri State area. There stood no fewer than five elementary schools from Bayonne New Jersey to New Milford Connecticut, called, "*The Stash Planski Elementary School*" because of the money he donated to start building those projects. There are also many parks scattered throughout the same three states, all bearing his name, due to his generous donations.

Well for the past three months, Stash had been fighting a losing battle with lung cancer. At first, he could get around somewhat, but as the disease infested his body, spreading from lungs to adrenal glands and liver, poor Stash became bed ridden and eventually was under the care of hospice.

So how do Petey and I fit into this picture? Simple. When Stash was admitted to the Telepathy wing of JFK Hospital, in Avenel, New Jersey, Petey was a volunteer candy striper there. She would go in and visit with the Planski's every day and they loved her company. One day Petey asked me to come and meet them, and I did. We instantly hit it off, and as often as I could, I would go up to visit my new friends the Planski's. As it turned out, Mrs. Planski was a heck of a chess player, and I loved the game too. So most days, Mrs. Planski and I would play chess and Petey would read or just talk to Stash. Even after Mr. Planski was released to go home for his final days, Petey and I were there as often as possible.

By the time Stash Planski passed, Petey and I felt like we had lost a member of our own family. Then about two months after the funeral, I got a call from Mrs. Planski. She wanted to have lunch with Petey and I. Arrangements were made and we had lunch at Harold's on Route 18 in East Brunswick. It was great to see Mrs. P again, and to just talk. Then she said that there was something she wanted to do for us, and she would not accept no for an answer. She said to pick the one place in America we would like to go for vacation, and she would foot the entire bill, and that we should live like "money was no object." Immediately Petey and I protested but Mrs. P would have none of it, saying,

"What you two have given me and Stash cannot be purchased for any amount of cash. I am only sorry that there isn't more I could do for you,"

So, yadda, yadda, blah blah blah, and Petey and I were headed for Vegas.

Somehow, the Human Interest department of Eyewitness News found out about the gift Mrs. Planski gave us, and the next thing you know, we were on TV.

They asked us all kinds of questions ranging from, "how did we meet the Planski's, to, "did we ever eat at Snausages, and what our favorite meal was," and finally, "what did we plan on doing on our trip to Las Vegas?"

We stated that we would be leaving the following Monday, spending three days at the Sands, the fourth day at the Grand Canyon, then two more days at the Sands, and finally home.

Well, that night, after the news broadcast, it seemed like my phone was going to explode from all the calls I received from people who saw us. It appeared as though everyone in the world was watching.

Chapter Two

Not Everybody was Watching

Although it felt like everyone on the planet was watching the news that night, well, that wasn't even close to being true. But, in a single bedroom apartment, above a magic shop, about a mile North East of the Strip in Las Vegas, was a devastated mother, with a gold tooth, who was watching. Watching, yes indeed.

Chapter Three

Crystal is Born

The next day I was back at work at a little music store called The Leg Band. Craig Brewer was the owner of the shop, and my boss for the past two years. Craig hired me as a salesman and guitar technician right out of high school. We met at a battle of the bands night where his band (The Leg Band, hence the name of his music shop), beat out my band, The Invisible Robot Fish, for first prize.

I ended up working at The Leg Band because my dreams of going on to college and playing football abruptly came to an end, when my good friend Marty Delorenzo accidently fell on me and tore my ACL in my left leg. Marty was the largest kid on our team and was playing right OT. Our quarterback fumbled the snap and I was the lone running back and the first one to fall on the ball. I don't know what the hell Marty was thinking, because I obviously had recovered the fumble and was curled up in the fetal position cradling the ball to protect it, when I felt Marty's massive girth come crashing down on top of me. I heard a pop as the ligaments in my knee were blown out. Right there and then my football career came to an end. I decided to give up college and pursue a career in music, which was one of the great loves of my life.

I was at my workbench in the rear of the store, adjusting a beautiful 1957 Gretsch 6120 with a Bigsby tremolo, when Petey came through the open doorway. "What's up Petey?" I asked as our eyes met for a brief second. Silence. Nothing. No response

whatsoever. She walked right past me and started looking at the

assorted guitars and basses in various states of repair lying on the

bench behind me. Again I asked, "Petey, what's up?"

It was the same silence as when the maestro taps his baton

on the podium and the entire orchestra snaps into position awaiting

the conductor's signal to start playing.

I stopped what I was doing, turned around and tapped Petey

on the shoulder.

"Petey, what's the matter, why are you ignoring me?"

"Oh, I'm sorry, were you speaking to me?" asked Petey.

I tried to remember if we still had any of the mushrooms left from

our party last Friday night that Delorenzo brought over, and

whether she may have taken some.

"You must have me confused with somebody named Petey,

however my name is Crystal."

Okay, so where was Allen Funt? Obviously Craig must have

called *Candid Camera* and at any second Allen Funt would be walking out of my closet. "Huh?" was all I could mutter. I must have looked mighty perplexed, because Petey couldn't keep a straight face any longer. She had this crazy laugh, "He, he, he, he," but it was the cutest thing in the world.

"It's me Chuck, Crystal!" exclaimed Petey. "Guess what, I've changed my name. I am sick and tired of people meeting me, and asking me my name, and when I say Petey, they always say, 'Oh like the dog in the Little Rascals?' I am sick and tired of being compared to a dog so I changed my name to Crystal".

"Ah, Okay," was all I could say.

Chapter Four

A Mother's Lament

For the first time in nearly two years, Brativa woke up feeling like her life had a

purpose.

Two years she had made the mistake that most of us share, and thought things could never get worse, after hearing the news that her eldest son, Jules, had been killed. Poor Brativa thought she had sunk to the deepest pit of pain and emptiness that any mother could endure. But then, when shortly thereafter she learned of her other son, Bradford's demise, *and* by the same hand that had taken Jules, Brativa reached a deeper level of gloom than most people could even imagine. The shock was so bad that she went beyond depression into darkness. Thoughts of getting any kind of help, or even of suicide, were light years away from the neighborhood in which a mother who lost both her sons was capable of living.

With absolutely no one or nothing worth living for, she just existed. One day about two weeks after they buried Bradford, Brativa took what little money she had left from her emergency stash (a Maxwell House coffee can containing around $7,000) and bought a one way plane ticket to Las Vegas because that was the first poster she saw when she went into the travel agency. She brought nothing with her, not even a toothbrush, nothing except all the newspaper clippings about her sons she had accumulated. When she landed at the airport she got in a cab and said, "Vegas."

The cab driver asked which hotel, but she did not answer. So he headed for the Strip and figured she would tell him more when they got there.

With about a mile to go to get to their destination, she saw a sign from the highway that read, Los Hermanos. She told the taxi driver to pull off, and he obeyed. As they entered the main street of the little dessert village, she saw a sign in the window of a magic shop reading, "ROOM for Rent".

So today, two years after renting her one bedroom apartment above *Houdini's Return* magic shop in the little village of Los Hermanos, Brativa felt like she could breathe for the first time.

It all started last night when she got home from her job as a dispatcher for the Canyon Lands Air and Land Touring Company. She kicked off her shoes, threw a chicken pot pie into her toaster oven, and sat on the couch to rewind her VCR so she could watch the latest episode of *Taxi*. Nothing really interested her on TV, but she thought Alex was a good looking man and Latka was funny. She always set the VCR to start recording about 15 minutes early just to be sure she wouldn't miss the start of her show, and also because she could catch a few minutes of the news which was on right before *Taxi*.

She knew that after all of the horrible bullshit that was on the news every night, they liked to end it with a feel good human interest story.

The first time *the story* played, Brativa just sat there with her mouth open as if the hinge holding her lower jaw had been broken. She did not rewind it and play it over again immediately; that would come later. For now she just hit the stop button and closed her eyes as endless flashbacks of her nightmare past came to the surface for the first time in a long time. She lost all track of time, and might still be sitting there in shock, but the smell of her chicken pot pie that now was on fire had reached her nose. She jumped up, grabbed a broom and swung at the toaster oven like she was Babe Ruth after he just pointed to right field.

The cord unplugged and the Apollo 11 toaster oven with its crew of chicken pot pie flambeau aboard made a crash landing in the middle of her kitchen floor. Brativa managed the small catastrophe, cleaned up the mess, and then went back to the couch to re-watch the news story about two lucky teenagers who had won a trip to Las Vegas.

The plan to kill the lucky teens did not even enter the heartbroken mother's mind at first. She just kept wondering where she went wrong. She tried to be a good mother. She always worked hard and cooked and cleaned and tried to help with their homework. Thoughts came and went like wind blowing through an open window, scattering important papers everywhere. Brad seemed always to be in trouble. He had a nose for it. On the other hand, until Jules was deserted by that piece of shit wife of his, his life seemed almost normal.

But how could she be mad at the innocent kids who murdered her boys? The papers said they were heroes. They even made the local news. It wasn't these innocent kids' faults that they were in the eye of the storm when her babies had their manic moments of overwhelmdon. What were the poor innocent kids supposed to do? "*Who knows and who cares*," she thought. For some unknown reason the universe had decided to bring these people all together at that precise instant of time, but...wait a minute, she thought. They *killed* my babies. Cold blooded. And then they were celebrating. What kind of animals celebrate killing someone's babies? No, that was bullshit. They were not innocent kids; they were fucking animals and they deserved to die. She even thought how perfect it would be if she killed herself after she killed them. Perfect. All ends tied up like a row of neat black hefty bags filled with autumn leaves and lined up along the curb to be picked up and disposed of, once, and for all. Yes, that was what made the most sense.

Chapter Five

God Damn the Pusher

Two hundred and sixty pounds of good natured, albeit, not by any stretch of the imagination, the most intelligent muscles, also known as Marty Delorenzo, had fallen asleep in his favorite chair.

But this was no ordinary chair. In fact, nothing in this one bedroom, basement apartment was what you would call ordinary. For starters, none of the four chairs, the couch or loveseat, had any legs. This was because one night while he was slightly stoned, Marty thought it would be a good idea to saw the legs off the furniture so no one would get hurt if they fell off when they were drunk or high. Usually his roommate, and my best friend, Joe Pensipine, would not agree with this childish type of thinking, but on that night Joe was also a little off center and he not only agreed, he enthusiastically helped.

What first hit your eye when you walked into their hippie pad was "the bar." Marty and Joe had built a bar made out of two by fours and paneling, to enhance the party atmosphere of the room. Their apartment had many other unique attributes. Worthy of noting was the hideous burnt orange drapes that were not hung on curtain rods above the windows, but rather just nailed to the walls. Opposite the curtains, behind the stereo, where most people would hang a large mirror or a nice picture, was a six foot rainbow, constructed out of used Ticketmaster concert tickets that were also nailed to the wall. The living room doubled as Marty's bedroom as well. (He slept on the couch with no legs). Both Joe and Marty slept with hammers in their beds to kill the ridiculously large insects that also liked to think of this basement apartment as home. Marty told me that on more than one occasion he had smashed one of these critters with his hammer, only to have it laugh in his face and scurry away. Even though I have found this hard to swallow, Pensipine backs up the story.

"Marty Wake Up," shouted Joe, as he simultaneously whacked the big lug on the back of his head. "Cops are all over the place outside and I think they are headed here!"

"Huh, what? Huh?" was all that Marty could muster in his half awakened state.

"The cops, three cars full, parked out front and I think they are headed here" whisper shouted Joe.

"Fuck -- why the fuck are they coming here? We aint done nothing." replied Marty who had already gotten to his feet.

"Because you're a fucking pusher, and we're going to jail, that's why," answered an excited Pensipine.

"Balls, balls, balls, and more fucking balls. I ain't no fucking pusher. I never made one cent selling pot. I mean, I sell it, but I don't make any profit. I just get the connects for my friends who can't obtain for themselves, but I aint no fucking pusher! So what do we do?" asked a slightly shaken and slightly overwhelmed Delorenzo.

"Okay, you stall them at the door, and I will get all our weed and flush it. Just don't say anything stupid, Okay?"

"Fuck you, you're the stupid one for thinking I'm a pusher."

"Fine, fine, you're not a pusher, your just a jerk who is going to jail for selling his pot for no profit," and with that Joe Pensipine headed for the bathroom with the weed.

Knock, knock, knock. Marty Delorenzo composed himself as best he could and opened the door. At first when he looked out he thought his eyes must be playing tricks on him because he saw nothing. Then he looked down and saw a girl of about ten or twelve years old, in a brown uniform, with her arms full of boxes looking up at him.

"Hello mister. I am Lauren and I am a Brownie and I would like to know if you would like to buy some delicious Girl Scout cookies," asked the little girl.

Poor Lauren did not know if the towering man in front of her was going to cry, throw up or pass out, but he just stood there staring at her.

"Mister, are you alright?" she asked.

There was nothing but a big stupid blank daze on Marty's face. Then he heard the sound of the toilet flushing, and he came back to his senses.

"Uh, no, sorry; no thanks, gotta go. Thank you, maybe next time," Marty said as he slammed the door in the little cookie pusher's face.

"Joe, stop! Don't flush, don't flush; it was a mistake!" Marty yelled as he went flying into the bathroom, where he found

Pensipine sitting on the toilet doubled over. At first Marty thought Joe was crying, but then realized he was laughing hysterically.

"What the fuck is so funny?"

"Oh, man, you should have seen the look on your face. You look exactly like you did when Herman Edwards scarfed up Joe Pisarcik's fumble back in '78."

Like condensation evaporating from your windshield from the warm dry breath of the defroster, things were becoming clear to Marty. Realizing the practical joke which had been played on him, he asked, "and the pot?" like a kid who wanted to know the fate of his puppy after hearing the poor pooch was hit by a car.

Joe held up the half ounce bag of Panama Red and was instantly engulfed in the big arms of Marty Delorenzo. "I don't know whether to kill you or kiss you for setting me up," blurted Marty, and for an instant Pensipine wasn't sure if Marty was going to squish him or start crying.

The two friends went back into the living room, put a pinch of the high grade marijuana in the old familiar bong and sat on the legless couch. "How lucky are Chuck and Petey?" asked Joe.

"Yeah, all they do is babysit some rich old fart for awhile and the next thing you know they are living the life of plenty," replied Marty.

"You're telling me, man I wish we were going to Vegas. Shit, we could win a crapload of money, not to mention the chicks."

"Fucking ay chicks and money, I could definitely use some of that," said Marty as he filled his lungs with the cool white smoke from his latest bong hit.

The boys sat quietly, contemplating for a few minutes, like Indians at a pow wow, as they passed the bong back and forth between them. They knew from experience that they did not need to do this too much, for their old friend, Miss Panama Red packed a pretty potent punch.

Joe Pensipine broke the silence. "Then that's it. We're going to Vegas. We will surprise them."

"And just how the hell are we supposed to finance this little extravaganza?" asked a Chinese eyed Delorenzo.

"Simple, my dear Watson, we will just sell a little bit of the fine *maryjane* we got here."

"Screw that" said Marty. "I told you a thousand times, I AINT NO PUSHER!"

"Money, gambling, chicks, adventure...c'mon man, just one time for the boys, think about it," pleaded Joe.

"Well, seeing as you put it that way, I guess one little time won't hurt."

Joe looked into Marty's glazed eyes and said, "God Damn, the pusher"

Marty looked back into the equally glazed eyes of his friend Joe Pensipine and said, "God damn, the pusher man." And with that they both rolled off the couch (thank goodness the legs were sawed off) and stumbled into the kitchen to eat some hot dogs and chocolate milk while they made up their plans for Las Vegas.

Chapter Six

Sin City

Organized crime, prostitution, easy marriage, easy divorce, show girls, corruption and gambling. Wow, what else could someone ask for? Wow, the city of a million lights. Wow. Although my travels thus far in my short life had been extremely limited, I have to imagine I would be hard pressed to find another destination that jolts my imagination or has the ability to make my fantasies come true, no matter what I am looking for, like Las Vegas. Even before my plane landed, my heart kicked it up a notch seeing the Strip materialize, as if almost out of nowhere, in the middle of the vast desert wasteland.

Petey, oops, I'm sorry, *Crystal* and I had barely stepped foot off the jet way before I found myself being drawn to the call of the slot machines, ringing, singing, blinking and practically calling my name, right there in the airport terminal.

Chapter Seven

The Sands

Reclusive and wealthy businessman, the legendary Howard Hughes owned two hotels next to each other on the Strip. We passed his other hotel, the Desert Inn, first. Then our cab took us right up to the front door of our hotel, the Sands. Holy mackerel, talk about a couple of fish out of water. Crystal and I were simply amazed by the glitz and enormous size of this joint. We had stayed at places before, but this was a far cry from the Howard Johnsons we lodged at. After checking in, the bell hop took our bags and guided us to our room. We passed signs directing people to the Copa Room. *The Copa Room* for God's sake. This is the place where the Rat Pack got their name. During a magical three week period in 1960, when filming *Ocean's Eleven,* Frank Sinatra, Dean Martin, Sammy Davis Jr., Joey Bishop, and Peter Lawford performed on the Copa's stage together for the first time. Wow, how cool must that have been? Not only did this place have a history of legendary entertainers, but it was once owned by mobsters like Meyer Lansky and "Doc" Stacher, and even Frank Sinatra had a piece of it.

If cool was somewhere you could visit, then the Sands was definitely cool.

So, as soon as we got into our room, Crystal announced she was exhausted and going to take a shower. I unpacked our huge valise.

While Crystal was busy soaping up the *Crystal Palace*, I finished putting our stuff away and was looking out our window at all the glitz up and down the strip.

Chapter Eight

Wang a Bang a Ding Dong

So as I looked out my window and thought about all the cool things me and Crystal were going to do, (we had already booked a night to see Don Rickles, and had also purchased a sightseeing tour of the Hoover Dam and the West Rim of the Grand Canyon) and suddenly my eyes started to focus on two familiar silhouettes. I looked, blinked, refocused and looked again, but I couldn't believe what I was seeing. Could that really be Pensipine and Delorenzo walking down the street towards the Sands? It couldn't be; could it? Now Joe Pensipine would be pretty easy to miss in a crowd, but Delorenzo, that big monkey, would stick out like Wilt Chamberlain at a midget toga party. As sure as the statue of liberty was the last nice thing the French ever did for the U.S., I was sure that at any moment my two buddies would be knocking on our hotel room door.

"Petey, Petey, er, I mean Crystal, you are not going to believe who I just saw walking towards our hotel" I said as I cracked the bathroom door open, to not only make sure she heard me, but also to sneak a peek at my beauteous girlfriend.

"Sinatra and Sammy Davis Jr.?" asked my girl, who had already wrapped herself in a white terry cloth robe and did that magical hair thing with a towel that all woman seem instinctively to know how to do so it looks like they are wearing a turban.

"No Mrs. Funny lady," I said. It is Joe and Mike.

"Yeah right Chuck, what the heck would those two be doing here?"

"I have no idea, but I think we are about to find out."

"I have an idea," said Crystal, with a devilish look in her eye. Let's turn the surprise on them."

"Okay Crystal, you have my interest, what are we going to do?"

"I think we should leave the door open a crack, and they will probably just let themselves in. Meanwhile, we can hide in the bathroom and scare the heck out of them when they come in."

So we quickly re-established our position in the bathroom. I also put on a white terry cloth robe and let Petey do the magical hair thing with a towel, to my head.

We listened eagerly for our unsuspecting prey; Petey and I were like primitive abominable snowmen, with our white terrycloth fur standing on end just waiting for the exquisite moment of unfetted satisfaction, when predator descends upon prey. A few seconds later we heard the rap of a knuckle on the door. We tensed, but did nothing else. Another rap, rap, rap, and another non- response. Finally, we heard the heavy door slowly open. Petey held up three fingers. She put one finger down at a time as she slowly mouthed the words, three...two...one and then we exploded from the bathroom like the maniacal Bulls of Pamplona.

"EIYEEE!" Shrieked a petrified, casually dressed woman, who jumped so hard from the fright of seeing us two lunatics spring toward her that she dropped the bottle of champagne she was carrying. She fell flat on her face and for a second Petey and I thought we may have scared her to death. I slowly rolled her over onto her back and I instantly noticed something was "different" about her. It wasn't the fact that she had a look on her face which combined sheer terror, bewildering shock, and maybe what could have passed for an itsy bitsy bit of hatred; no, it was the fact that this woman had one gold tooth.

Chapter Nine

The Fifth Wheel

It was as if I were one of those horrible little stuffed animals crammed inside a glass box in a boardwalk arcade in Asbury Park, where you spend twenty dollars in quarters to maneuver a toy mechanical crane so you may get lucky enough to snatch one of these useless treasures, just to impress your girl. But instead of a metal crane pulling a ragamuffin up into the air, it was the big paw of Delorenzo yanking me effortlessly off this poor woman.

"Chuck, what the hell is going on here?" asked a confused Marty D.

"I spotted you and Joe heading our way while I was looking out the window, so Crystal and I were going to scare the crap out of you guys when you came in, only, somehow this poor woman got here first."

"Are you alright lady?" asked Joe Pensipine as he helped the victim of our miscalculated assault to her feet.

Brativa quickly gained her composure, brushed the surprise off her blouse and slacks, put a smile on her face and held out her hand as she introduced herself in a very heavy Russian accent.

"Hi, I Betty and you must be Chuck," she said, as she took my hand and shook it. Somehow, when she grabbed my hand it felt as if I had just shaken the hand of death. Although her mouth smiled her eyes were like looking into some scary ass place, "And who might your friends be?" she asked.

Although questions were formulating in my brain, like, who are you and why the hell did you just walk into my room, I decided to answer her question first before asking her my own questions. After all, I did just nearly scare the Dickens out of her.

"Well as you know, I'm Chuck, this is my girlfriend Crystal, and those are my best friends, Joe and Marty."

It took all of Brativa's strength not to pick up the closest object and smash the skulls of this entourage to a bloody pulp. These maggots had cold bloodily murdered not one, but both of her children. But two thoughts stopped her. First, it was unrealistic that she would be able to accomplish this skull smashing here and now in this hotel room. After all, the big monkey Marty could squish her like an annoying pimple before she could get much damage done.

But another question came to her mind -- one that troubled her deeply, because it might throw a huge kink into her morbid plans.

Who vas dis girl Crystal, and vere vas de other one, Chuck's girlfriend Petey? Did he break up vith her? Is this his new girlfriend? Ven did this happen? After all, It vas not long ago that I heard the story about Chuck and his girlfriend Petey being such wonderful Samaritans that the vidow of sausage king, Mrs. Planski had rewarded these brats with dis trip. And as much as I vanted the rest of these brats erased from the surface of the planet, I did not vant to hurt an innocent girl.

Poor Brativa. Poor, poor Brativa. She always was a good mother, she loved her sons. Yes she killed her asshole husband Sean, but he deserved it, didn't he? Oh, wait, I forgot, he *accidently* fell out the window, that's right. Oh dear God, why were things always so blurry. How come things never turn out the way they are supposed to? Get married, have children, and live happily ever after. You know why? Because my dear friends, life is not fair. As a child you are told tons of bullshit including that the cops and politicians are good people. But the biggest lie of all is that life is

fair. Just ask the innocent mullet swimming somewhere in Upper

Tampa Bay if it is fair that an osprey just plucked his fucking ass out

of the water and he is now in excruciating pain as he hangs from

the osprey's talons, if life is fair. Fuck no; it is not fair. It is what it is.

So what was poor Brativa to do? She wanted to kill these piece of

shit baby killers, but who the fuck was this Crystal? Fuck, always a

God damn monkey wrench to complicate things. Okay, somehow

she would have to get Crystal out of the picture before she killed

the other ones.

"Very nice meet you, although not exactly velcome I'm used

to," said Brativa as she quickly composed herself. Sorry, sorry, sorry

came the choir response of my entourage.

Her eyes smiled but were projected by a black heart.

"As I say, I am Betty, and I vork for Canyon Land Air and Land

Touring Company. I vill be taking you lovely childrens to the Hoover

Dam and the Vest Rim of the Grand Canyon. I brought a bottle of

Champagne courtesy of Mrs. Planski. I vill pick you up tomorrow at

8 a.m. at the main entrance. I am sure ve vill have a great day.

Good day children." Marty, Joe, Crystal and I shook Betty's hand

and she left the room.

Although Crystal and I didn't smoke pot on a regular basis,

today was anything but regular, and the entire gang got high,

compliments of Marty.

Mrs. Planski had given me $5,000 dollars (with the

stipulation this money must be used for gambling), to have fun with

at the casinos while I was there. So, stoned as hell, our gang headed

to the casino floor. I gave Marty $1000 and I gave Joe $1000 and I

kept $3000 for me and Crystal. Now, my favorite type of gambling is

Texas Holdem' poker; however, that would be no fun for Crystal, so

I decided to try some craps first. That didn't work out so well, so I

went to my second favorite type of gambling which is Black Jack.

Petey, (whoops, sorry Crystal) and I played for hours, drank for

hours and finally went back to our room – broke, but drunk as hell. I

laid on the bed and Crystal went to the bathroom.

The next thing I knew, my angel came out of the bathroom wearing a pink bra with slits in it so her nipples were poking through. Her panties matched, and also had a slit in them, to allow access to the object of my affection. In other words, she was hot. We put on some music and Crystal danced for awhile as my eyes devoured her like a gourmet dish. Finally, she danced over to the bed and we spent the next couple of hours as one. At last, exhausted, we lay in bed, her head on my chest as I caressed her body. "Petey, ooops, Crystal, I love you," I whispered.

"And I love you Chuck," she responded.

So we passed out in each other's arms and were awakened by a knock on our door. We threw some clothes on and I answered the door. It was Joe. "God damn," he said, "I was doing so good, I don't know what the hell happened. I was playing Black Jack and one minute I was up as hell and the next thing you know I was broke. Fuck me. Damn it. Just once I wish luck would roll my way."

"Aw, don't worry about it Joe, I hope at least you had fun, I mean it wasn't your money, so don't sweat it. We are still going to

Hoover Dam and the West Rim. Just relax buddy, it is all good," I told my best friend. He tried to put on a happy face but was failing miserably when our hotel room door flew open. In a blur we saw Delorenzo and two fists full of money explode into our room.

"FUCKIN AYYYYYYY!" screamed Delorenzo. "Thirty-two thousand fucking dollars!! God Damn, I say thirty two thousand dollars, that's what I won. I have *thirty three* thousand dollars counting what you gave me Chuck."

In my entire life, I had never seen a happier person. The big monkey just jumped in bed with us in his exuberance. Pensipine looked like he was in shock. So Crystal says, "Holy crap Mikey, how did you do that?"

And he says, "Fuck if I know. I was just pumping money into the nickel slot machine and then all of a sudden, Bingo! Bells are flashing and an attendant comes up to me and takes me to the cashier window and the next thing I know I am fuckin rich!"

"Holy shit" is all I can manage to say. Joe is doing some kind of crazy dance like he is secretly listening to some wild groovy song on *Soul Train*.

So out came some more herb, and room service was called. (We ordered champagne, lobster, and steak, and that was just for starters). And this evening my dear friends, we lived like the crowned heads of some damn country or another.

Finally, Joe and Mike showed themselves out and headed back to their room. Petey and I resumed where we left off before the jackpot festivities began and I traveled down some roads that before this glorious evening, had never been traveled before, and we fell asleep in each other's arms more crazy in love than ever.

Chapter Ten
Oliver's Army

CHORUS:
Oliver's army is here to stay
Oliver's army are on their way
And I would rather be anywhere else
But here today

There was a checkpoint charlie
He didn't crack a smile

But it's no laughing party
When you've been on the murder mile
Only takes one itchy trigger
One more widow, one less white nigger -- Elvis Costello

All that night Brativa kept hearing the lyrics to Elvis Costello's "Oliver's Army" in her head. "But it's no laughing party, when you've been on the murder mile. Only takes one itchy trigger -- one more widow, one less white nigger." Oh goodness gracious, was she on the murder mile? Was she one more widow with an itchy trigger finger?

"Vat da blazes has happened to my life?" wondered Brativa. *"Yes, it vas never really easy. Oh my stars, lordy knows I have seen my share of hard times, but for da love of One who created all, am I really going to kill three childrens tomorrow? For heaven's sake, dey have der own mothers, and how absolutely devastating vould that be for dere poor mothers."*

No one knew better than Brativa what it was like to lose a child. For the Blood of Jesus, she had lost two. Lost? Really? Is that what happened? Did her children go for a walk and then just suddenly disappeared? Or did some cock-sucking spoiled rotten piece of dead dog shit kill her babies? Chuck the fucking Devil Kikel killed all that was precious to her. Okay it was true; Bradley was a tough cookie, but her eldest son, Captain Jules... Captain, in the name of the Father, Son and the Holy Ghost, her son was a Captain. He was a good man. He didn't deserve to die like a slaughtered pig on his own God Damned Boat. Fuck You Chuck Kikel. FUCK YOU! Die you unholy, unworthy, unearthly black cloud of a human. I am going to fucking kill you, I am going to fucking kill you, I am going to fucking,,,,,and then she passed out, thinking, *"And I would rather be anywhere else but here today."*

Chapter Eleven

Morning Glory

Oh what a glorious morning. I couldn't help but sing one of my favorite songs off the White Album, *"The sun is up, the sky is blue, it's beautiful and so are you, Dear Crystal, won't you come out and play."*

"I thought we were back with Petey?" inquired my sleepy eyed lover.

"You know something, beautiful? I think the name Crystal is starting to grow on me," I said as I rolled over, spooned my girl, and lost myself in her soft and pretty smelling hair.

"Well I think..."

BANG, BANG, BANG on our front door. I scrambled out of bed, threw on my robe, (man I loved my complimentary robe), and ambled toward the door.

"Throw open the floodgates," barked the voice of my best friend Joe Pensipine.

"A little friggin' early, wouldn't you say so Joe?" I asked as Joe and Mike entered our room.

"You kiddin? At the buffet downstairs, me and Mike already had enough breakfast to make our sides explode," said Joe as he flopped down on the couch.

"And besides, that Betty chick said we had to meet her at eight," chimed in Delorenzo as he also slunk down onto the couch.

"Okay, okay, you two go downstairs and let Crystal and I get ready. We'll meet you at the main entrance about ten minutes to eight"

So they left and Crystal and I hopped into the shower and then got ready for our adventurous day at Hoover Dam and the Grand Canyon. Little did we know that the adventure we were anticipating and the adventure that we experienced would be as different as a Steppenwolf vs. Liberace concert. Liberace was beautiful, graceful, melodic, relaxing, and just made you feel nice and warm all over. Steppenwolf was like getting hit in the face with a steel frying pan while at the same time riding the rollercoaster at Coney Island.

Chapter Twelve

Steppenwolf

Get your motor runnin'
Head out on the highway
Looking for adventure
In whatever comes our way

Yeah, darlin' Gonna make it happen

Take the world in a love embrace
Fire all of your guns at once
And explode into space

The Canyon Land mini bus was waiting for them as they rounded the corner of the building.

Chapter Thirteen

The Beginning of the End (How fitting for chapter 13)

Betty/Brativa pointed the mini bus east and headed down East Flamingo Road, toward interstate 515 west. Then followed a 300 mile journey to the West Rim of the Grand Canyon, a place that Chuck and his crew would have absolutely added to their bucket lists, had bucket lists even been invented way back then.

Chapter Fourteen

The Mojave

I remember thinking to myself, "*There are actually people who don't like the desert.*" They think it is empty, vast, dead and boring. They couldn't be further from the truth. The desert is one of the most beautiful panoramas your eyes will ever lay sight on. Every color of the prism cascades itself, sprawling across the windswept sands of time. Joshua trees and cactus of every shape and size prickle this magnificent landscape as far as your imagination will take you. So I sat gazing out my window as we journeyed along. Crystal was in the back of the mini bus grabbing a beverage. In the meantime, up front, Mike Delorenzo was showing Joe Pensipine the weed he smuggled to Vegas, which he had wrapped up and taped inside his blue jean cuffs.

All of us were kinda lost in our own worlds. This was a lucky break for Brativa. If we weren't, one of us might have found it odd that our tour guide, *Betty,* hadn't spoken one word to us over the mini bus microphone. Not that that bothered us or anything. But if we had thought about it, we would have wondered why she hadn't said something like, "Good morning everyone! I hope all of you had a great night sleep in Sin City and didn't stay up playing too late. Are there any big winners on the bus? Does, anyone know what type cactus we just passed? Look out the right side and you will see a roadrunner just off the side of the pavement." You know typical tourist / tour guide banter.

Not that there wasn't a conversation going on full speed inside Brativa's head. Questions and random thoughts were pouring through her mind like the waters of the Hoover Damn going through the huge turbines. *"Should I kill dem all or should I let Crystal live?After all, she has noting to do vith dis. How far should I go before I kill dem? In which order do I kill dem? Am I really going to shoot a bunch of kids? I have to pee. Okay, I am going to let Crystal go, but how, and vere?"*

It was really a good thing none of us were paying any attention to our driver, or we would have noticed that even though the mini bus was a very comfortable 75 degrees, Brativa was sweating profusely. There were dark sweat rings peeking out from her underarms, and her brow and top lip were dotted with beads of sweat.

As Brativa was internally wrestling with so many different decisions, she suddenly saw a roadrunner cross the road about fifty yards in front of the mini bus. At first she was not convinced it was even real. Maybe it was just a mirage, just like the endless array of little pools of water on the black, baking asphalt, which were continuously disappearing just as you approached them, were a mirage. Then she figured, mirage or not, that was the sign to get the show started.

She checked her rear view mirror to make sure no one was in sight and then suddenly, pulled the mini bus over to the side of the road.

Betty stood up, turned around, and announced, "Very sorry children. I need terribly to make a stop. I tried to vait for ladies room, but unfortunately, I vill not make it. Crystal darling, vill you please come vith me? There are many snakes and scorpions in desert, so I vood like you to keep a lookout. You others, please do not look, as dis is embarrassing enough. It will only take a moment." With that, Brativa got out of the vehicle and waited on the driver's side for Crystal to come around and meet her. She wasn't positive Crystal would follow, but thought, *"if I just go and don't vait for* qvuestions, she vill come." And Brativa was right. Crystal looked at me, giggled, and went to watch Betty pee.

Brativa was flying without a net. She never really planned the details of how all of this was to get done. Now she started to worry," what if da boys do vatch me pee, after all, all men are fucking pigs. The boys vill vatch, my plan vill be over, and I vill just shoot myself." But no more time for thinking, just time for doing.

When they reached about thirty yards away, Brativa crouched down, tugged down her pants and began peeing. Perfect. Not only did she get to release her bladder, but there was Crystal two feet in front of her with her back turned toward the pee-er. Brativa stood up, pulled up her pants, and said, "Crystal, sweetie," where upon Crystal spun around, only to be punched smack between the eyes by a perfect right hook. The world went dark and Crystal collapsed to the ground. Before any of us on the bus realized what was happening, our tour guide from hell jumped back into the driver's seat and gunned the gas. Brativa had no idea how young and resilient Crystal was, because Petey was only a few steps behind Brativa when she got into the bus.

What happened next was like a blur. Bradford B. and Captain Jules T's mother drove for about ten seconds. Mike, Joe and I were just starting to comprehend that something was terribly amiss and we were about to leave our seats and make a mad dash for our suddenly lunatic tour guide, when Brativa slammed on the brakes, throwing us into the seats. Meanwhile, Crystal was doing her best Jesse Owens impression, and running as fast as she could for our mini bus. Brativa sprang out of her seat, and before any of us could reach her she produced a gun and started screaming, "You bastards have three seconds to lay on top of each other on floor or I start shooting. One, two," and like obedient dominos, we were all squished and wedged on top of each other on the floor. Without another word, Brativa hopped back into the driver's seat and took off. She bent the rear view mirror so she could watch us, and as she did she noticed that if that last stop took one second longer she would have had to deal with Crystal again. Crystal was only steps away from the bus when Brativa pulled away.

To Brativa Terwilliger, formerly Brativa Domotuski, mother of Bradford B. and Jules Terwilliger (both deceased, or more in point of fact, both murdered), it seemed like someone had taken time and put it in a blender. Ten minutes seemed to take ten hours *and* ten seconds at the same moment. She didn't know how long she had been driving, so she depended on her instinct to know what to do. Again she swerved the little bus to the side of the road. There was nothing but desolate tract for as far as the eye could see. Again the gun was pointed at the laundry pile of boys on the floor, and Betty ordered us to slowly get into the last three seats. Without removing her stare from us she reached into a paper bag by the driver's seat and grabbed a handful of handcuffs. She knelt down on one knee and slid the cuffs back to us, saying, "Each of you handcuff your self to your seat." After this was done, she came back very cautiously to make sure we were all secure. I thought about a sneak attack, and grabbing Betty as she walked by, but the risk of her getting a shot off and possibly killing one or more of us was just too risky, so I remained still.

Brativa thought to herself, "*Vhy don't I just kill dem right here and now? No one is around, It would be over in flash, and den… yes, and den…,*" True , it was the *den* that had her baffled. … "*Den just throw da bodies on side of road? Drag da bodies into desert and bury them?*" No, these ideas just didn't seem right. Besides, she wanted these brats to know why they were going to die. So she decided to take them all the way to the Grand Canyon, where she would cruise down West Rim Drive until she got to Pima Point. She would either kill them there or go a little ways farther to Hermit's Rest. On second thought, she would go all the way to Hermit's Rest. From there she would go down to Hermit Creek Campground and then finally hike to the Colorado River for the Grand Finale'. This would allow her to have time to tell them all why they were about to die. Also, it would be fitting and convenient to dump the bodies into the Colorado River.

Chapter Fourteen

Flirtin' with Disaster

I'm travelin' down the road and I'm flirtin' with disaster
I've got the pedal to the floor and my life is running faster
I'm outta money outta hope it looks like self destruction
Well how much more can we take with all of this corruption

-- Molly Hatchet

So Joe, Mike, and I were trying to figure out what the hell was going on. Betty seemed to be lost in her own thoughts and was paying little attention to us. After all, she had us locked down pretty tightly with the handcuffs she had picked up at Houdini's Return, the little magic shop below her apartment.

"What the fuck?" were the first words whispered out of Mike Delorenzo's mouth. To which Joe Pensipine and I had the same reaction, raised eyebrows and raised shoulders.

After a few seconds of thought Joe said," At least I know Petey is alright, I saw her running after the bus." To this statement we all nodded our heads in agreement.

"Do either of you have any idea who this Betty woman really is, or what she has planned for us?" I whispered to my friends.

"Not only can I not answer that question, but also, why the hell did she throw Petey off the bus?" asked a very confused Joe.

"Do you think she wants to have sex with us, and that is why she got rid of Petey?" whispered Mike Delorenzo.

"Shut the fuck up," answered me and Joe in a tandem whisper. I guess we both whispered this a little louder than we thought, because Betty snapped back at us without even turning her head, "No, you all shut fuck up. No more talking. I answer all your questions soon enough."

The boys and I decided there was no use trying to pull a *routine six,* right now. For crying out tears, we were pretty helpless at this point. So we figured we would sit tight and wait for a better opportunity to go routine six.*

Luckily, Brativa had made this trip many, many times before while working for the Canyon Lands Air and Land Touring Company. On occasions when there were large groups going to the Grand Canyon, Brativa went along to assist the driver and tour guide. Except for piloting the helicopter or the tour boat, Brativa had done it all. In fact, she knew this National Park almost as well as anyone. She knew when the best time to book a tour was. She knew who the best operators to work with were. She also knew when certain areas were closed due to things like floods or repairs. This last bit of information was all she needed to formulate the rest of her plan. Brativa knew that the trail from the Hermit Creek Campground to the Colorado River, the 1.6 mile Dripping Springs Trail, had been closed to the public due to dangerous footing from recent floods. Perfect.

*Dear readers—if you recall from our first adventure, "Blood on the High Seas," routine six, or routine any other number for that matter, was what Slip Mahoney or Satch Jones would yell to the rest of the Bowery Boys, whenever they were in a desperate situation and would resort to a premeditated plan to help get them out of a jam. They had routines for everything. So, when the boys and I go routine (fill in any number), it just means all hell is about to break loose, so do your creative best to be part of the team and overthrow our opponent. CK

Chapter Fifteen

The West Rim

The stone slab read, "The Grand Canyon *WEST,* Home of the Hualapai Tribe, *Gamyu* ! Welcome !"

Everything seemed like business as usual to anyone watching the Canyon Lands mini bus pass the entrance to the West Rim of the Grand Canyon. That is, everything looked normal except the fact that everyone in the bus (including the driver maybe), would probably be dead soon.

The scenery was spectacular as we passed Pima Point, turned on to Hermits Road and finally came to a stop at a stone arch which had the words "HERMIT'S REST" hand printed across one column of the arch. Betty shuffled through some things around her driver's seat, situated her back pack, put her gun in her hand and came back to unlock her prisoners. But before she reached us she stopped dead in her tracks as if she had walked into some invisible wall.

"My name is not Betty" she spoke softly, yet with a heavy Avenyian accent, "And I am not tour guide from Canyon Land Tour. My name is Brativa, and I am poor and lonely vidow. My husband died accidently years ago. Oops, did I say died accidentally? Excuse me, I'm sorry. I meant to say 'Vhen I pushed abusive son of bitch out vindow" she thought and chuckled at this thought, but there was absolutely no humor left in her. She just seemed to stare at the floor of the bus. It appeared as though she was looking through the floor, through the dirt and directly into the bowels of hell. And then she looked up, directly at us, and with tears in her eyes said softly, "I also lose two sons, but this no accident. This vas cold blood murder."

We could almost feel the heat radiate off of Betty, I mean Brativa, as her face turned red with anger. "Murdered," she almost whispered with a deep guttural growl. "And by who vere my boys murdered," she continued as she walked closer to us, "By teenage animals who don't care that dey tearing a mother's vorld apart. Lousy, stupid fucking teenagers who think it must be joke to kill someone's children."

Joe Pensipine and I could feel our stomachs tighten up and churn like a washing machine, because already we were pretty sure we knew where this conversation was going. Mike Delorenzo, on the other hand, was totally oblivious as to where this was headed and was very intrigued and moved by the story. That was, until Brativa's next words left her mouth and found their way to our ears.

"I am going to uncuff you from seat. Then put your hands behind back and I recuff them. When I done vith first, valk out and lean against bus until I finish vith other two boys. They too vill valk out one by one and lean on bus. If anyone decides to run before I am done, don't you vorry, I vill shoot your friends in head immediately, then I come for you. Understand? "

It was at this point that I believe Delorenzo finally understood the situation. His expression changed from sad and empathetic to HOLY SHIT, she is going to fucking aye kill us!

Well, Mike Delorenzo was the first one of us that Brativa freed from his seat and recuffed. Mike D. walked slowly to the front of the mini bus, stepped down the two black rubber covered steps, and hit the ground running. Now I've seen the big boy run during football or baseball games, but I had never seen him truck like this. He bolted like someone had stuck a lit candle up his ass. Before any of us could say anything, he was gone, somewhere behind the rocky outcrops that surrounded us.

Joe and I looked at each other in total disbelief. That stoner had done some pretty dumb things in his life, but never would either of us believe he could pull a stunt like this. Run to save himself and leave us to die? Unimaginable.

It took a few seconds for it to register that we weren't dead yet. We looked at Brativa. If this situation wasn't so deadly, I think Pensipine and I would have laughed at her. She just stared out the window and slightly cocked her head to the side, and looked like a puppy that just heard a high pitch sound he couldn't quite identify. But that only lasted a few seconds and then she lifted her gun, pointed at us, and said, "Get off de fucking bus."

Chapter Sixteen

My Gran Pappy always would tell me, "Boy, even you and a blind n...."

"Now wait awhile, wait awhile, before we head on back down to the river for some more fine fishing, I needs to makes me an appointment with Mother Nature. Ya' all hol' tight and I'll be right back."

Man, this was better than Harold the Hillbilly could ever imagine in his wildest imagination. Even though he spent ninety nine percent of his life growing up hunting, fishing and living in the beautiful Catskill Mountains of New York State, he had always dreamt of going to the Grand Canyon and fishing the Colorado River. And now, finally, his dream had come true. He'd saved up enough money to stay in a little cabin just outside the Grand Canyon, and to hire a guide to take him fishing. He couldn't afford a private fishing charter, so he opted for a group charter, containing four other people and a guide.

Harold stood up and brushed crumbs of the vestiges of his delicious shore lunch; fried cut throat trout with baked beans, and buttered cornbread, prepared exquisitely by the group's guide.

Then he walked a short distance down a gravely narrow path and ducked around an outcropping of canyon wall. He was almost done relieving himself when he heard footsteps approaching from above him on the trail. As he was not completely finished peeing, he stumbled off the path and into the scrub brush to finish the task at hand. He wanted to stay concealed for two reasons. He did not want to startle the hikers, and he didn't want to explain what he was doing. Just as the newcomers came into his camouflaged viewpoint he finished his business and started zipping up.

"Holy Mother Joseph and Brother Jesus!" he silently screamed inside his mind. Was that really Chuck and Joe, *handcuffed,* and walking in front of some woman with a *gun*? Could it be? Could it *be?* Hard as it was to believe, yes, in fact, that was what was happening.

"Now wait awhile, wait awhile," Harold's mind raced. He knew he better do something and do something quickly or else this new apparition of an unimaginable trio would be stumbling upon his little fishing party, and then for sure all hell would break loose.

"*Okay,*" Harold thought. "*I am going to circle behind them, use the the the element of surprise and grab that there woman from behind. At the same time I'll grab the pea shooter from her hand and turn the bastard on her, my new prisoner,*" his thought concluded.

So, as simple as this old friend's plan was, it probably would have worked except for one little overlooked factor. As soon as Harold took step number one towards his goal of a sneak attack, molten hot red bolts of toxic venom were injected into his ankle by a pair of needle sharp fangs attached to the business end of a six foot Western Diamondback rattlesnake. What happened next could probably be mistaken for a comedy if the ramifications of the outcome weren't so deadly.

At the same time as Harold was screaming in equal parts of pain, fear and surprise, Joe, Brativa, and I nearly jumped out of our skin as this bolt from the blue caught us equally unprepared and off balance. Joe and I immediately fell to the ground and rolled into the fetal position determined to protect ourselves as best we could.

Let's face it, our nerves were already stretched to the max,

anticipating a bullet going through the back of our heads at any

moment. So when we heard Harold the Hillbilly scream, we had no

time to think; we just reacted and fell into survival mode.

Simultaneously, Brativa, also not expecting or knowing what

the primal shriek meant, fell over backwards and landed with her

gun and feet pointed straight up in the air, like a dead cartoon

animal if it died pointing a gun at God. For the next few moments,

the only sound or movement was from Harold the Hillbilly's

attacker slithering away towards the safety of some nearby rock

pile. Still silence. Joe and I were afraid to even breathe. We realized

we were not getting shot, but could not imagine what the hell was

going on. Because of the way Brativa fell, she could see the snake as

it made its non ceremonious exit, and also see Harold as he writhed

in pain on the ground just a few short yards from her. She finally sat

up, got to her knees and then to her feet and walked closer to the

strange man behind her.

"Wh, wh, wait a while, wait a while, pl, pl, please help me,"
begged Harold. Upon hearing this strange, yet familiar, dialect, I
lifted my head and questioned "Harold?" At this moment, Joe
Pensipine also raised his head and also questioned, "Harold the
Hillbilly?"

At this point, Brativa's mind was somewhat of a cross
between *The Twilight Zone* and *The Outer Limits* TV shows.

"Vat de fuck is going on here?" demanded a bewildered
Brativa, her voice quivering as she continued, "You know dis man?"
she directed at Joe and me.

"Ch, Chuck, Joe, la la lady, please help me," implored a now
slightly shivering, slightly sweating, and totally petrified Harold the
Hillbilly".

"You *know* dis man?" repeated Brativa, only a little more
intensely now.

"Betty, er, I mean Brativa, there is no time for explanations
now," I said looking directly into her deeply confused eyes. I
continued, "We must get this man to a hospital instantly or he will

go into shock and die. Whether *we* know him or not is entirely non consequential. What is important is we get him some help right now. He has nothing at all to do with what is going on between us, so it would be a sin to just let him lay here and die."

I realized as I was saying this, that this might be the only chance of Joe and I surviving. I was pretty sure at this time that any 'Routine Six' attempt would probably fail miserably. I just hoped two things. First that my plea worked on her, and secondly, that she did not remember who Harold the Hillbilly was, and that he also had a large role to play when it came to killing her son Bradford Terwilliger with burning marshmallows.

For another moment there was silence and I was not sure what to think. Did she fall for it? Was there enough goodness still living within Brativa to not allow a total stranger to die because of her? Was she going to suddenly remember reading about Harold the Hillbilly and kill us all? Was she going to help Harold and still shoot Joe and me? Time froze and stood still, except for Harold the Hillbilly rapidly deteriorating a few feet away.

Poor Brativa's mind kept getting bounced around like that little white square ball in the ancient video game pong. Back and forth, forth and back. Her poor kids, *these* poor kids, poor Brativa. And then finally, and without warning, she decided the only thing she could do was put a bullet right through her brain and end all of her suffering. The pitiable woman's face went blank without expression. She lifted the heavy weapon to the side of her head, just above the temple, and pulled the trigger.

Chapter Seventeen

Hitchin' a Ride

A thumb goes up, a car goes by
Won't somebody stop to help a guy (gal)
Hitchin' a ride, hitchin' a ride
I've been away too long from my baby's side

-- *Hitchin' a Ride*
Vanity Fair

Fortunately, Petey's nose wasn't bleeding and her right eye never puffed up or darkened, despite the pain her face was in. In fact, if the blow she had received compliments of Betty's fist had happened in almost any other time or place, she would probably still be lying on the ground weeping about her situation. But Petey was a very smart girl, and she instinctively knew that she better act quickly or her boyfriend and his two best buddies could be in a deep heap of shit. She looked all around and saw nothing but desert from horizon to horizon. She decided the only thing to do was to walk in the same direction that the mini bus was traveling and hope, hope, hope, that sooner rather than later some kind of ride would come along.

Petey had walked for what seemed like days before she heard the distant sound of a vehicle approaching. Immediately her thumb went out as she turned her back towards the crazy lady and her three hostages who were rapidly increasing the distance between themselves and her.

"Cheese *and* rice, is that what I think it is," blinked Ira Feldheim, the elderly bespectacled man with exquisite snowy white hair and perfectly sculptured moustache, sitting behind the wheel of his six month old Cadillac Coupe De Deville .

"Excuse me dear?" queried his petite, yet surprisingly pretty for her age wife, who was sitting comfortably in her own plush leather bucket seat.

Until then, Mrs. Feldheim had been mesmerized looking out of her side window at the vast nuances and myriad of subtle changes in the colors and textures of the desert. Then she focused her eyes down the road, and confirmed that Ira did indeed see what he saw. It was a woman, rather a young girl, hitch hiking way out here in the middle of nowhere.

"What in tar nation is that girl doing hitch hiking way the heck out here all alone?" was the question from his wife Bernice's lips.

"I don't know" answered Ira.

"I can't imagine" answered Bernice.

"Should we stop?" asked Ira.

"Of course," answered his wife.

"Cheese *and* rice," stated Ira.

As the Gatsbyesque couple approached the stranger, they saw an expression of relief plus urgency spread across the young girls face.

"Need a ride?" asked Bernice through her rolled down passenger seat window.

"*Need a ride? **Need a ride**?*" No, I am just airing out my armpit while I get a spectacular suntan on my thumb," was what Petey would have said if circumstances were different, but instead she just nodded her head and said emphatically, "Yes!"

She hopped in the back seat, and prepared herself for the barrage of questions that were sure to attack Petey from her new septuagenarian friends. So to combat this, she figured the best thing to do was take the initiative, make up some cock n bull story of what she was up to (after all, she didn't want to alarm this obviously nice and sweet old couple.) She was thankful they stopped to help her and that was enough.

So she concocted some cockamamie story about how she accidently fell asleep inside some rest area and missed the bus which the rest of her cheerleading squad was already on and were heading to the National Cheerleading Championship being held later that day at the West Rim of the Grand Canyon. There were more holes in this tale than a big box of donuts, but Petey hoped that her new traveling companions would just accept the goods they were being sold.

Not only did the Feldheims buy the story, they bought the bridge too. To confirm this, Ira was more than willing to accommodate Petey by dramatically increasing his driving speed when Petey informed him she was afraid that she was going to be too late for the competition and blow a once in a lifetime opportunity.

At breakneck speed they darted toward their destiny.

Chapter Eighteen

No, No, No, No, Nooooo !

Ira had somehow managed to catch up to the deserted mini bus on the side of the road. Petey had somehow managed to ditch the Feldheim's.

She walked a little until she found herself waiting in ambush watching the tumultuous events unfold before her very eyes. She had waited as quietly and patiently as she could behind a rock ledge. Then, suddenly Betty started leveling the gun at her own head. Petey instantly launched herself with all her might at the possessed woman. Amazingly, as Petey flew through the air, her arm hit Betty's hand just as Betty squeezed the trigger. The gun exploded into a cacophony of sound, accentuated by the higher pitched twing of the rouge bullet ricocheting off one of the nearby canyon walls.

Petey opened her eyes and her first thought was that Betty was dead. There was blood all over the left side of her face and she lay motionless. Then after a few seconds she noticed Betty's chest rising and falling and knew the woman wasn't dead after all. Before she could let out a sigh of relief, she heard some disturbing sound coming from her left side, the direction where Chuck and Joe were standing next to Harold the Hillbilly, whose condition was rapidly deteriorating. Harold's breathing was shallow, deep and gurgled, as if the entrance to his windpipe was blocked by tumbleweed. His ankle was now very swollen and dark blue and purple veins were starting to migrate towards his heart. But what was that sound? It reminded Petey of something that a cow, sorrowful and full of woe, would chant: *moo, moo, mooo*. But that wasn't exactly right. Then her hearing started to recuperate from the sound of the gunshot and she realized that it was Joe Pensipine mumbling, no, no, noooo! She stood up to see what the hell was going on, and a horror which she had never felt before filled her heart. For a moment she thought she would faint, and then she did faint. A few seconds later when she started to come around, the world was still spinning. She looked over at Joe again and still could not believe her eyes. Her beloved Chuck was collapsed in a heap at Pensipine's feet, his entire head engulfed in blood. Chuck Kikel lay motionless -- partially in the dry grass, and partially on the gravelly path. What apparently happened was, when Petey tried to save Betty's life, she

inadvertently redirected the trajectory of the deadly bullet to

ricochet off the canyon wall and directly into the head of the single

most important person in her entire world.

As if this scene wasn't bizarre enough already, what

appeared to be two seventy something hobbits had just jumped out

of their Caddy and were bouncing down the hillside towards all this

mayhem.

Chapter Nineteen

Fade to White

A few days later, Harold the Hillbilly was re-positioning

himself in bed in the ASTU

(Arizona State Trauma Unit) wing of St. Stephen's Hospital in

Northeastern Arizona. The surgeons were able to save his foot and

leg, and although he would need some rehab, he was no worse for

wear.

"Now wait awhile, wait awhile, but Chuck, if you aren't

gonna finish dat puddin, would you mind very much tossing it over

here?" bemused Harold.

I looked down at my lunch tray and realized I had hardly touched a thing. I was just replaying all of the crazy events that had just happened a few days ago over and over in my mind.

Five minutes ago Petey had just stepped out of my room to go to the bathroom. But this morning she filled me in on everything that went down. She told me that the luckiest thing that ever happened to her in her life was the Feldheims coming around when they did. She didn't know it at the time, but Ira Feldheim, excuse me, Dr. Ira Feldheim, was a retired neurosurgeon from Johns Hopkins Hospital. His wife, Dr. Bernice Feldheim, was also retired from thirty five years of being an internist, also at Johns Hopkins. (In fact, the hospital is where they met and fell in love). The couple always traveled with a medical bag filled with all kinds of goodies, just in case, and in this case thank goodness they had. They quickly recruited the aid of the others and assembled a makeshift M.A.S.H. unit. Dr. Ira attended to me first since I was the most seriously injured and at the same time Dr. Bernice stabilized Harold. Betty/Brativa's wound was merely superficial so they left her for last.

There was no need for anyone in our group to call for help. The reverberation of the gunshot brought park rangers almost immediately and they called for Air Rescue and an ambulance.

****

The sound of someone knocking on the door brought me back to the present and I looked up to see Mrs. Stash Palanski, Mrs. Sausage Queen if you like, standing a few feet away. In her hands were beautiful flowers.

"Mind if I come in?" Mrs. Palanski asked.

"No, not at all," I said, with a big smile on my face. How ironic that we met when Petey and I were visiting her husband in the hospital, and now she was visiting me. I introduced her to Harold, and we all started chatting our heads off. Moments later Petey was escorted into our room by Joe Pensipine on one arm, and Marty Delorenzo on the other.

"And just where the hell did you disappear to Benedict Arnold? And what the hell were you thinking? I mean, you do realize you could have gotten me and Joe killed?" I asked Marty.

However, it was Joe Pensipine who cut in with the answer.

" Aw Chuck, we can't be too upset with the big ape. It turns

out he figured the *only* chance any of us stood of surviving was if he

ran for help. The problem is he was running so fast that he tripped

over some rip rap, smacked his head when he fell, and was out cold.

The great and extremely lucky part is, that when he came to, he

immediately crossed paths with the Feldheims. Lucky for you and

Harold he knew exactly where to bring them without wasting

another precious second."

"True Marty? I asked. And with that the big guy came over

to me and gave me the most gentle bear hug of all time.

We all sat around shooting the breeze for awhile, and then

something remarkable happened. Two uniformed Arizona

policemen escorted Brativa into our room. It got so quiet you could

hear the heartbeat of a flea in New Mexico. After looking at each

one of us, Brativa took a half step closer and said softly, "Sorry."

Tears started welling up in everyone's eyes, even Delorenzo's, but it was me who spoke next. "Brativa, you have nothing to be sorry for. What happened between us and your sons was so very unfortunate, and so senseless, and it is I, who should be saying sorry to you. Sorry those things had to end up this way. Sorry, that there weren't any other solutions at the time. And, I am especially sorry that you lost your children. I can't imagine how difficult life must have been for you for the past few years. Anyone in your shoes would have probably acted the same, under the circumstances. However, you actually never did anything wrong. When the moment of truth arrived you turned the gun on yourself and not us. You never hurt any of us."

Then I walked over to Brativa, put my arms around her and said, "I feel I can speak for the group when I say we will not be pressing charges against you, and if you wouldn't mind, we would like to keep in touch with you."

At this point the tears were really flowing, and Mrs. Palanski cut in. She walked over to the handcuffed woman and took hold of her hands. "Would you do me the pleasure and join me this Christmas at my home in New Jersey? In fact, I would like all of you to join me. And don't worry about money; I will pay for the entire stay for everyone."

With this Brativa could not contain herself any longer and performed one of the most awkward hugs you ever saw in your life to Mrs. Palanski. (You know, awkward because she was handcuffed.)

Then, from someone, somewhere in the room, a single voice started singing, "For he's a jolly good fellow." Naturally, the rest of us joined in.

The End

Chuck
Kikel
January
4, 2014

Made in the USA
Columbia, SC
24 January 2018